THE BRICK MAN

Lock Down Publications and Ca$h
Presents

THE BRICK MAN

A Novel by *King Rio*

Lock Down Publications
P.O. Box 944
Stockbridge, Ga 30281
www.lockdownpublications.com

First Edition October 2021
Printed in the United States of America

Lock Down Publications
Like our page on Facebook: Lock Down Publications @ www.facebook.com/lockdownpublications.ldp
Book interior design by: **Shawn Walker**

Stay Connected with Us!

Text **LOCKDOWN** to 22828 to stay up-to-date with new releases, sneak peaks, contests and more…
Thank you!

Submission Guideline.

Submit the first three chapters of your completed manuscript to ldpsubmissions@gmail.com, subject line: Your book's title. The manuscript must be in a .doc file and sent as an attachment. Document should be in Times New Roman, double spaced and in size 12 font. Also, provide your synopsis and full contact information. If sending multiple submissions, they must each be in a separate email.

Have a story but no way to send it electronically? You can still submit to LDP/Ca$h Presents. Send in the first three chapters, written or typed, of your completed manuscript to:

LDP: Submissions Dept
P.O. Box 944
Stockbridge, Ga 30281

DO NOT send original manuscript. Must be a duplicate.

Provide your synopsis and a cover letter containing your full contact information.

Thanks for considering LDP and Ca$h Presents.

This book is dedicated to Yvette Scott and Donta Parker

Huge shout to Ca$h and everybody at Lockdown Publications. I know I haven't gotten a chance to interact with the majority of you, but you'll soon see that it's all love when we meet. I'll be home in a matter of months!

To the readers, especially the devout ones — like Pam and her daughter in the Bronx, New York, and my doting aunt Denise who's somehow managed to read just about everything I've released — I thank you all for the support. I'm no longer able to comment on posts and engage with you the way I used to, but I'm on my way home very soon, and (God willing) we'll have ample opportunity to meet at book signings and other literary events. I'll most definitely be attending all of them, or at least as many as I possibly can. I love writing gangsta books more than I love reading them. Thank you all for allowing me to share my stories with you and your loved ones.

Family, y'all already know how I'm rockin' lol. I have a lot of releases on the way, both new and old, and I intend on publishing them in rapid succession until my entire catalogue is available. I hope there truly is a such thing as Heaven, and that Grandma Shirley and Granny Sarah are smiling down on me, at the optimism-driven Black street fiction writer I've become. Can't wait to rejoin my people in the land of the free. Especially my siblings and cousins; God knows how deeply I miss them.

To the bruddas, free y'all! Free Young Meach, P.A.T., Luck Ghost, Lilbeezyeanna flamedup westuptillyoufessup (AKA my mfn nucca Lil B!). RIP Red D, Neal Wallace Jr., Lil Luke, Lil Cholly, Bay Bay, and Lil Mark and all the other bruddas. Bankroll Reese, keep doin' it! Shout out everybody off 15th and Trumbull. I miss you, Chicago! Free Baby Mike, bro from 42nd and Post. Free Me.

Contact me on Facebook: Author Rio

Or via mail:

Mario Bardlette #120178

Branchville Correctional Facility

21390 Old State Road 37

Branchville, In 47514

Undying Love, King Rio

Prologue

Chicago, Illinois

Monday, July 4th, 2016

It was approximately two thirty in the morning when the first kilo arrived.

Thirty-four-year-old Lee "Juice" Wilkins was sitting in his red Cadillac Deville up the street from Chandra's house on Drake Avenue, sipping from a red plastic cup of cognac and listening as she described the size and shape of some girl she'd met at a club party last night.

"Man, Juice," Chandra was saying as she sat next to Juice rolling a blunt, "shorty was so fuckin' strapped. Ask Trav and Ceno. They were on her when she first walked in. Say her name was Melinda. She from the Dominican Republic, half black, half Dominican. Came out here for her uncle's funeral this weekend. He was one of the Stones from out south. Got whacked by some GD's somewhere out on 63rd..."

Chandra's ramblings went in one ear and out the other; although she was slim and pretty and thick where it counted, a bisexual little redbone nympho in her early twenties who'd been one of his sexual partners for about a month, the only thing on Juice's mind was the kilo.

Juice had been copping ounces of cocaine for going on a year now, cooking them with baking soda and selling the hard rocky substance to the drug addicts in the North Lawndale neighborhood, but this was his first time purchasing a whole kilogram. He was getting it from Hector, a fat Mexican guy he'd served time with in Stateville Correctional Center seven years ago.

He watched Hector's black Mercedes SUV as it rounded the corner onto Drake Avenue. It wasn't flashy like Juice's whip; unlike the customized Cadillac, which had chrome 26-inch Forgiato rims and candy paint, Hector's SUV was all factory. It pulled up behind the Cadillac and parked.

"I'll be right back," Juice said, opening his door. He was a wide and lighter-complected Black man in dark designer shades and a white True Religion outfit. The .40-caliber Glock pistol on his hip protruded from the waistline of his loose-fitting jeans. His white Air Force One sneakers were new and spotless. The cash in the Nike shoe box under his arm was all he needed to buy the kilogram of cocaine.

Hector watched Juice closely as he approached the SUV and pulled open the passenger's door.

Juice noticed the tight stare, but he trusted Hector and was more focused on keeping his eyeson the dark street around him. Over the past few years homicides in the North Lawndale neighborhood had skyrocketed. The local gangs were at war, and they weren't just killing their rivals; innocent men, women and children were being killed simply for being in the wrong places at the wrong times. Robberies were at an all-time high. The youngsters were obsessed with rocking the flyest designer gear, and a lot of them were willing to get it by any means necessary.

As soon as Juice was seated in the SUV he handed Hector the shoe box, inside of which was

$34,000 in cash.

Hector didn't even bother to count the money. He'd done enough business with Juice in the past to know that every dollar would be accounted for.

"Next time we meet somewhere else," Hector said. He tossed the shoe box onto the backseatand then reached back and grabbed a dark gray backpack. "I don't like it out here anymore. My wife tells me it's dangerous. I listen to her. She's a wise woman." He paused for a moment and then added: "She used to drive a mail truck out in Englewood. I made her quit the day a guy pulled a gun on her. This was when I first got out. You hadn't hit the streets yet."

Juice nodded his head and again glanced around the dark street. There had been a couple of street lights on Drake a while back but they were eventually shot out by the young guys.

There were two teenage boys standing at the corner of 16th and Drake Avenue. (All theother young gang members were at Red Diamond tonight, attending a Dreezy event). Their streetnames were Head and Lil Dave. Both of them were gang members, Head a 4 Corner Hustler, Lil Dave a Traveler Vice Lord like Juice. The two gangs were essentially one and the same in North Lawndale, and they were at war with a faction of the Gangster Disciples, the New Breeds, and the Black Souls, all three of which were notoriously violent street gangs.

The opposing gangs were serious threats.

Lately there'd been so many shootings, so many killings. Eight teenagers and two older guys had lost their lives in North Lawndale in the last month alone, and there had been just as many revenge murders in the neighborhoods of their enemies.

"It's safe with me around." Juice adjusted the gun on his hip. "We got choppas around this muhfucka. I feel bad for the nigga that wanna come through here on bullshit. Niggas gangbangin' too hard around here."

Hector didn't look too believing. He'd spent his fair share of time in the streets. He knew how dangerous minority communities were in the ghettos of the Windy City. A man could be shot for nothing more than resembling a rival gang member, or for wearing a watch, ring, or chain that cost too much.

Hector opened the bag, and to Juice's surprise there were two duct tape wrapped bricks inside it.

Two kilos.

"I'm fronting you one for twenty-five. That should last you until I return. I'll be out of town for the next week or so. Gotta head down to Sinaloa and straighten out some things with my people. That okay with you?"

Juice couldn't repress the grin that grew on his face as he realized that he was getting a second kilo for $9,000 less than Hector's usual price. He'd be able to sell the kilos for $40,000 apiece or break them down and make around $75,000.

Of course Juice could also cook the kilos into crack and have his gang push the dope for him. This way he'd make a sizable profit and also make sure his team was eating.

Putting off the decision until later, he flicked his eyes around, checking out the area for the umpteenth time tonight.

He was zipping the backpack shut when a blue minivan suddenly appeared at the corner of 16th Street and Drake Avenue — where Head and Lil Dave were standing.

The minivan's sliding door swung back, and the barrel of an assault rifle eased out of the darkness within.

Then there were gunshots.

Lil Dave and Head drew guns from their hips (Dave still had a revolver he'd robbed a man for last week, and the Mac 11 submachine gun Head had belonged to Juice), but the shooter in the minivan opened fire before Head could get off a shot, and Dave only got off one before hetoo was riddled with bullets.

Juice pushed open the passenger's door, snatching the bulky pistol from under his shirt and watching in horror as high-caliber rounds from the assault rifle tore through the bodies of Lil Dave and Head.

The minivan sped off before the two boys hit the ground and disappeared faster than it hadarrived.

Shocked by the brazen attack, Juice stood with one foot in the SUV and one foot on thecurb, gawking at his fallen soldiers.

"So," Hector asked, "you sure it's safe with you around?"

Chapter 1

To Juice's knowledge, there were five witnesses to the double homicide on 16th and Drake Avenue: Juice, Chandra, Hector, Candy, and Brianna.

The latter two eyewitnesses were cousins. They were curvaceous young strippers, coming home after a long night on the pole at Redbone's. They had been stepping out of Brianna's small black BMW when the first gunshots sounded.

Candy and Brianna were born and raised in the North Lawndale neighborhood. They'd been around Juice and the other older gang members for most of their lives. Candy was twenty-one, and Brianna was twenty-two. They were the kind of girls that made everybody stop and stare. Absolute dime pieces.

Their closeness to the Lawndale mobsters was what compelled them to run across the street to Juice instead of rushing off into Brianna's house. Candy screamed out for someone to call an ambulance as she sprinted along behind Brianna. They made it over to Juice's side just as a Mercedes Benz SUV was veering off from the curb.

Juice handed the backpack to Chandra and said: "Come on, everybody in the house," and the four of them headed up the street. He glanced back and saw Apple, one of his guys off 15th and Trumbull, swiftly approaching the bodies. The first thing Apple did was snatch up Lil Dave and Head's guns. He seemed to be checking Head's pulse when Juice turned back to the girls.

Three houses down from Juice's car was Chandra's place. She lived on the first floor of a red brick duplex building. Someone had left a torn blue shirt on the concrete stairs that led to the front door. It seemed to be the most unlikely thing for a balanced human being to trip over, but at the moment Brianna wasn't the most balanced person; she had taken Ecstasy and Molly at the strip club, along with several shots of Louis 13 de Rémy Martin and a few lines of the white stuff. The five-inch Giuseppe heel on her right foot somehow became tangled up in the shirt. She stumbled and fell against Juice's back as everyone was entering Chandra's place.

He glanced back at her and kept moving. He was so focused on securing the kilos that he didn't stop to think of the smear Brianna's makeup-covered face had left in the middle of his back.

In the living room, he told everyone to stay there while he went to Chandra's bedroom and stacked the kilos in the steel safe he kept in her closet. He shut and locked the safe and then closed the closet door. He didn't realize he still had his gun in hand until he returned to the living room.

"They ain't movin'!" Candy said, peeking through a curtain at the crime scene out front. "Jesus Christ, Juice. They're dead!"

Juice joined Candy at the window. A part of him wanted to run outside and lend some sort of help to the wounded boys, but he didn't wanna be caught with a gun by the police. Especially not after what had happened to Alton Sterling in Baton Rouge a couple of weeks ago.

Especially when he had two whole kilograms of cocaine in Chandra's bedroom

"Chandra, turn off all the lights," he said. "Let's all just sit in here and kick it for an hour or two. Police will be done came and left by then."

As if on cue, sirens began screaming in the distance. Flashing blue and red lights zipped pastthe window.

Juice and the two stunningly beautiful and shapely young strippers sat down on the sofa while Chandra rushed around the house turning off lights. The sofa was an aging brown leather mound of comfort. Juice had fallen asleep on it many a days.

When there was only one light left on — a shaded lamp on the end table nearest Juice — Chandra took a seat on Juice's knee and let out a despondent sigh.

"I know who shot them," Brianna muttered. "I know whose minivan that was. I just saw it atthe store when we stopped to get some blunts. Big Jay and Darren was in it. We went to school with them. They're Breeds from off 13th. Shit. I can't believe that shit just went down like that."

Juice soaked up the information without uttering a single word. He texted Kev, a nephew of his who was also his second in command, and revealed what had just happened to Head and Lil Dave and what he'd just learned from Brianna. She snuck a fleeting glance at his phone as he composed the text, but she said nothing. He figured she was probably worried that perhaps she'd said too much, worried that maybe she'd be the next shooting victim for working with Darrenand Big Jay's opps.

"Fuck them niggas, sis," Candy said as tears rolled down her pretty, yellow complected face. "Lil Dave is my nigga, man. That shit's fucked up."

From the flashing lights illuminating the street out front, Juice guessed that there were four or five more Chicago Police Department vehicles on the corner. He was nervous, but not afraid. He'd been through it all in this neighborhood, with the police and with opposition members.

He put a hand on Candy's shoulder and gave it a consoling squeeze. He too was hurt, but he didn't show it. Juice hadn't shed a tear since his best friend Cup was killed last year, and before that it had been a dozen years since he'd cried.

Nowadays, gangsters in Chicago didn't shed tears. They shed blood.

When the police presence out front became too overwhelming, Chandra led the way to her bedroom, stopping in the kitchen to grab her bottle of Hennessey out of the refrigerator and four cups. Everyone sat down on the bed. Brianna fell back, kicked off her heels, and gazed up at the ceiling.

"Don't start throwing up and shit," Candy said, wiping the tears from her face and looking back at Brianna.

"Nuh uhh, not in my bed." Chandra pointed to the door. "Make a right then a left. That's the bathroom. Or if you can't make it there I got a trashcan next to the bed. Whatever you do, don't throw up on my shit."

"I'm fine, I'm fine," Brianna said, stretching out the words. Like Candy, she wore a small belly shirt, tiny denim booty shorts, and several rings and necklaces. She had her smartphone in one hand and a large shoulder bag under her arm.

Juice was pouring himself a half cup of cognac when Brianna suddenly sat up and raced off to the bathroom. Seconds later, the sound of her vomiting gave everyone twisted expressions.

Candy went off to comfort her friend.

Resting her head on Juice's shoulder, Chandra sniffled and said, "That dumb ass girl just told you who was in that minivan. You're about to go nuts. I know it. I know how y'all do."

"Big Jay and Darren," Juice said, nodding his head and rubbing his chin between thumb and forefinger. He didn't say more, because there was nothing more to be said on the matter. Darren and Big Jay were going to get dealt with for shooting down two of the guys.

"What was in that book bag?" Chandra asked.

"Stay out of grown folks' business. Where my blunt at? Since you wanna start asking questions."

"I dropped it in the car when they got to shooting. Shit, I was scared outta my mind. I can't believe they caught Lil Dave lackin' out there. You know everybody's about to go nuts over that. Wait until they get back from the club and see what done went down out here. I feel for their asses." Chandra went in her purse and found a sack of potent marijuana.

Juice and Chandra were soon rejoined by Candy (Brianna stayed in the bathroom). The three of them smoked a blunt and drank to the memories of Lil Dave and Head.

The girls reminisced about the times they'd shared with the two boys. Candy had once dated Head a while back, and both her and Chandra had messed around with Lil Dave; Chandra and Candy had been in the same class with Head's older sister; and Lil Dave had one of Chandra's cousins eight months pregnant with twin girls.

Juice didn't join in on the reminiscing. He could think of nothing but the two kilos.

Chapter 2

Darren and Big Jay abandoned the minivan on 13th and Christiana and then walked a block over to where two of their fellow mobsters — B Man and Cash Boy — were waiting in the alleyway on Sawyer.

They were in B Man's mom's car, a clean gray Pontiac Grand Prix with a donut for its rear driver's side tire. Big Jay got in the backseat with the AK-47 concealed in his baggy jeans. Darren got in next to him and immediately delivered the news.

"We just smoked them hoe ass niggas on Drake," Big Jay said. "Lil Dave and some other nigga. Nailed em to the ground with this choppa, on Black Gangsta."

B Man was rolling up a blunt. He said: "Hold up. Let me flame up this Lil Dave pack right fast."

The gang laughed at that. They were glad to have gotten some revenge for the murder of BigJay's sister, who'd been accidentally shot and killed by a TVL during a drive-by shooting two weeks ago.

The war between the Black Gangsters (New Breeds) and the TVLs began over a simple fightbetween two men more than eight years ago, and since then there had been at least forty killings directly tied to the ongoing dispute. Darren had survived being shot four times last summer. He'dseen the gunman run out from beside his house. He'd tried to run, but the bullets had knockedhim down. By the grace of God, his attacker's gun jammed when the man stood over him and attempted to finish him off. If not for that miracle he was certain that he'd be just as dead as the mobsters he'd just watched Big Jay shoot up.

After smoking a few cigars full of Kush, the gang split up and went their separate ways, promising to hit each other up first thing in the morning.

Darren lived with his grandfather in the apartment right below Big Jay's mom's apartment. He agreed to hide the assault rifle in his bedroom for the night and ended up putting it under his bed before stripping down to his underwear and lying down.

For a while he gazed into the dirty, rotating blades of the fan next to his bed. He tried earnestly to shift the weight of guilt off his shoulders. In middle school and high school, he had attended classes with Lil Dave. He knew Lil Dave's mother, had in fact gotten a ride from her once. His ex-girlfriend, Jokisha Blackshear, was Lil Dave's cousin.

"Had to slide on em, though," Darren said aloud to himself. He'd watched Lil Dave hang outthe window of one of the three cars that shot up 13th and Sawyer last night. It was also rumored that Lil Dave had killed J-Ro and KJ, two 17-year-old New Breeds that were murdered within hours of each other a couple of days ago. If Darren and Big Jay hadn't caught up with Lil Dave when they had, he was certain that his gang would have suffered even more casualties.

Darren picked up his HTC smartphone from the floor next to his bed and disconnected the charger. He had a text message from a girl he'd been fucking whenever his dick got hard. Her name was Shaila, and she lived in the apartment one floor beneath his. He was just about to replyto the text when the smartphone rang with a call from her.

It was no surprise to him that Shaila was awake at this time of night. She and her two sisters were known cokeheads. They were known to be up all throughout the night, visiting cocaine dealers and liquor stores, turning up with two dozen or more equally turnt up young black girls.

"What up?" Darren answered, sitting up and plugging in his ear buds.

"Nigga, you know what's up. I'm on my way up there...unless that hoe up there with you. Is she up there?"

The "hoe" Shaila was referring to was Jokisha. She hated Jokisha with a passion. If not for Jokisha, she felt that she and Darren would have been engaged to be married a long time ago.

Darren told her that Jokisha wasn't around. In fact, about a week and a half ago, he and Jokisha had called it quits. She knew he was cheating on her with Shaila and another girl. Thelast straw was last month when she'd found a used condom next to his bed. Since he and Jokisha had never used protection, she had easily figured out what was going on and left him that day.

Now, thinking back, he decided that ending the relationship might have been a good thingfor both him and Jokisha. He had just participated in the murder of her favorite cousin. (He felt certain that it was murder, after having seen Dave's head practically explode from the impact of an AK-47 round). He figured Jokisha would be trying to set him up to get whacked if they were still together on this particular night. Especially if someone ran their mouths about the shooting.

Darren wasn't about to be the one running his mouth. When he walked Shaila into his bedroom a moment later he didn't even think to mention the shooting.

It was Shaila who brought it up.

"You hear about what just happened to Lil Dave?" she asked as she poured a small pile of coke onto the cover of a Wahida Clark book on his dresser. She shook her head. "I know you don't get down with dude n'em anyway but still...it's fucked up. All this shit is fucked up. Everybody wanna talk about how much black lives matter, but I'm more worried about gettin' shot by a nigga than I am a cop. It's gettin' so crazy out here in these streets. We gotta stop lookin' at each other like we're the enemy. That's the reason black folks ain't got shit now."

Shaila shook her head again. Clad in a short brown pair of shorts and a white crop top shirt, her skinny body was sexy to Darren in a runway-model kind of way. Her white Air Force One sneakers were clean and fairly new, with just one little scuff mark across the back of the left shoe. She was one of those skinny girls that had a nice handful of ass to hold on to. If not for her drug habits Darren might have scooped her up a long time ago.

He walked up behind her as she was snorting a line of coke, pulled out his thick penis, and placed it on her ass. She began moving back and forth, slowly and gently, looking back at him and smiling.

She turned to face him. He put a hand on the top of her head and urged her to her knees.

Shaila had just flickered her tongue on the crown of his dick when the sound of a door beingkicked in frozen them in place.

It sounded close, but Darren knew that it wasn't his grandfather's front door.

"This is the Chicago Police Department! Jason Duncan, we need to come out with your hands in the air!"

Darren gasped.

Big Jay was busted. For Lil Dave's murder? For one of the other shootings that had taken place over the past few years? Darren didn't know what was going on, but he hoped like hell that he wasn't going down next.

Chapter 3

Chandra was the kind of girl that sucked dick like she was born to do it. She could deep throat, she could use her hands or go hard without them, and she had the most talented tongue Juice had ever seen.

He watched her suck and lick and spit on his dick while he thought of his wife, Shakela Wilkins, and the trouble he'd be in if she ever found out he was cheating on her with Chandra. Especially since Shakela and Chandra had been neighbors for several years when Chandra was a preteen. Her and Chandra's mom were close friends. They worked together as massage therapists in Orland Park and occasionally went clubbing together.

Next week would mark the one-year anniversary of Juice and Shakela's marriage. Shakela was under the impression that he was staying at his friend Rell's house for the night. He hoped and prayed that she wouldn't come through and check to see if he was there.

Juice rubbed his heavy brown hand on Chandra's naked butt and took in a deep, satisfied breath. All that could be heard were the wet slurping sounds coming from her mouth. Candy and Brianna were fast asleep on a blanket on the floor at the foot of the bed.

Saliva from Chandra's wet mouth trickled down the sides of Juice's dick. He felt the wetness on his scrotum. The glowing red numbers on the digital clock next to the bed read 5:32 a.m., and Juice was dead tired, though he and Chandra had slept soundly for a couple of hours. He couldn'twait to get a nut off so he could go back to sleep for at least another hour or two.

The sound of explosions in the distance reminded Juice that today was the fourth of July. Hehad a family barbecue planned for the holiday, and about a grand worth of fireworks he'd be setting off for the 18-year-old twin daughters and 17-year-old son he had with Shakela.

Just as he was getting ready to bust a billion more sets of twins in Chandra's mouth, Candy's pretty face rose from the foot of the bed.

Juice liked Candy. He knew that her ass and breasts were about as real as a three-dollar bill, but it all looked good on her and he'd been wanting her for quite a while.

"Y'all couldn't wait for us to pass out," Candy said with a laugh. She shook her head and put her hands on her hips.

"Girl," Chandra said as she stopped sucking and began sliding her tongue up and down the length of Juice's dick, "you don't even know. I was ready to thot it out right there in the car before all that crazy shit went down."

"Can I join in?" Candy asked.

A huge grin spread across Juice's face. He most certainly had no objections.

"Yeah, it's cool." Chandra giggled at the look on Juice's face. "I'm sure he won't complain.

We were just getting started anyway." "Sure won't," Juice agreed.

He dug in his pocket for a condom and tore it open. Chandra rolled it on while Candy peeled off her short-shorts and joined them on the bed.

Chandra rode him first. Reverse cowgirl. Her pussy was sopping, as usual. Tight and warm and inviting. Juice gripped her waist and chewed on his bottom lip. Candy ran the palm of her hand across his chest and belly. She too was biting her lower lip. Her eyes were glued to his phallus as Chandra bounced up and down on it, moaning and groaning and pushing her breasts together.

"Look at you," Candy said, smiling. "Fat-belly ass boy."

It was true that Juice had an oversized belly. He wasn't a fat guy by any means but he was definitely on the heavier side. On his forearms the words "Holy City" were tattooed in large cursive letters, and "Rest Up Cup" was inked in an arc on his belly to symbolize the undying love he had for his slain friend.

He really enjoyed it when Candy got on top of him. Although her ass was fake, it felt real, and it was about twice as large as Chandra's. He squeezed big handfuls of the meaty derriere cheeks. His smartphone rang twice on the bedside table with calls from his wife but he ignored it. He would return the call as soon as this little sex session was over.

Candy's moans were loud enough to awaken Brianna, who got up and hurriedly rushed off to the bathroom without hardly giving the threesome a second look. By the time she returned Juice was taking off the condom and skeeting a hefty load of semen across Chandra and Candy's wobbling derrieres.

Brianna rested her forehead on the open door and sighed. "Hurry the fuck up, Candy. We gotta get cleaned up for the video shoot," she murmured weakly.

Beaming, Chandra looked back over her shoulder at him. "Nothing like an early morning threesome," she said, slapping a hand on one of Candy's phat cheeks.

Chapter 4

An odd feeling swept through Juice as he drove past the spot where Lil Dave and Head had been shot dead on the corner of 16th and Drake Avenue.

Seeing the bloody squares of sidewalk was a sobering reminder of how real things were in the streets. There was a war going on, a gang war of turf and manhood, revenge and respect. Nobody was safe.

The drive to his and Shakela's house on 13th and Central Park Avenue took all of twenty minutes, but that was only because Juice was in no hurry to get home. He made a stop at McDonald's for four breakfast burritos and an orange juice, all of which were gone by the time he pulled up in front of the house and parked behind his wife's cherry red Escalade.

During the drive, he'd sent a text message to his nephew Kev and told him to be here as soon as possible. One of the kilos was in the trunk; Juice was going to cook it up into about 44 ounces of crack-rock and give it to Kev to have the young guys serve it under his watch. Juice planned to pocket at least a grand off every ounce, leaving plenty of room for Kev and the young dealers to make some cash for themselves. It was a win-win for everyone involved.

The kids were still asleep when Juice got in the house, and Shakela was at the kitchen table seasoning the meats — steak, sausages, hot dogs, beef Angus burgers, and chicken — that they would be barbecuing shortly.

Juice leaned in and kissed his beautiful wife on the side of her face. Shakela was thirty-five, a year his senior, and she still looked just as stunningly beautiful as she'd looked when she was twenty. She had on a pair of blue jean shorts and a pink halter top under an apron. Her hair and nails were perfectly done. Her rich brown skin was silky smooth, and she smelled about a thousand times better than the food seasonings.

Shakela's shape had not been a factor in Juice's decision to marry her, but it certainly was a plus. She was buxom. She had thick thighs and an incredible amount of ass. But what had drawn Juice to her was the undeniable fact that she had style and grace and was the most loyal, kind- hearted woman he'd ever met.

Shakela gave him the side eye as he went to the fridge for a cold beer.

"Where'd you stay last night?" she asked. "I told you where I stayed. At Rell's spot.""So, Rell wears makeup now?"

Juice turned to her and frowned. "What?"

"There's a whole face of makeup in the middle of your back. Where'd it come from? Rell?"

Juice took off his shirt to see what Shakela was talking about. There was lipstick on the backof his shirt. It took him a moment to remember where it had come from.

"Aw," he said.

"Aw?" Shakela moved to grab her hips, then didn't; she had all kinds of grease and seasoning on her fingers. Her pretty brown visage churned into a scowl.

"That was—" he paused, staring at the smeared makeup, digging through the memories of last night "—Lil Dave and Head got killed last night. Some girl ran into me when we ran off."

"What do you mean 'some girl'? You know every-damn-body in Holy City. What's her name? What's the bitch's name? Tell me so I can go and ask her about this makeup incident."

Juice tossed the shirt onto the seat of a ladder back chair at the table. He put his hands on Shakela's waist and drew her in to him.

"I don't know who it was, baby." Juice tried using his most convincing tone of voice. He pecked his lips against Shakela's, studying her frigid expression in hopes of warming it over. He kissed her twice more, once on each cheek, and filled his mammoth hands with her ass.

"Don't try to sweet talk your way out of this, either. I'll fuck you and that bitch up." A slight smile grew on her face. She rolled her eyes up to the heavens and let out a tremendous sigh.

"I'll find out her name and give it to you. Wait until Kev gets here. I'll have him find out. 'Cause I don't be knowing all those young girls."

"Mm hmm." Shakela gave him another eye roll, but she was breaking.

"You shouldn't be tripping over themselves, baby," Juice said. "I only have eyes for you.

Didn't I tell you that on our honeymoon?"

"Yeah...You did." She sucked her teeth. "And the next day you had those loyal ass 'eyes' glued to another bitch at my job. My best friend's daughter, at that. So you can miss me with that,too."

"Are we about to turn this holiday into an argument over nothing?"

Squinting tightly at her pot-bellied hubby, Shakela returned the kiss to his lips and then turned around and got back to preparing the meats.

Juice put on a very brief smile and quickly left the kitchen for the bathroom across the hall from their bedroom. Once there he hopped in the shower without stopping in the bedroom to get his outfit ready. He had to be quick. He'd soaped and rinsed his dick in Chandra's bathroom sink before heading out, but Shakela's sense of smell was similar to a K-9's. He remembered one time when he had bumped into an old schoolmate at the mall. They had shared a hug and a few words; Shakela had detected the woman's perfume as soon as he returned home.

It was a good thing that this was his week to do laundry. He'd have the white True Religion outfit washed and dried and folded up in a drawer before wifey had time to accuse him of anything else.

He dropped the dirty clothes in the laundry basket. In the bedroom, he changed into a red summer outfit by the same designer. (Here lately, Juice's affection for the designer brand had essentially turned his closet into a True Religion store).

He put on a fresh pair of red and white Jordan sneakers and a New Era fitted cap with the Bulls logo on the front of it. After checking himself out in the bathroom mirror, he dialed his nephew Kevin's phone number and jogged back down the stairs while the phone rang. He was on the fifth stair from the bottom when Kev answered, which is where he sat down to talk in private.

"I'll be pulling up in a couple minutes," Kev said. "Got Tara and Poochie with me. We hadto make a few stops."

"Yeah, It's all good. I just got out the shower. We ain't even started cooking yet."

"Tara whipped up some potato salad and a big ass pan of cheese spaghetti. I brought some more cups and plates, too. We still had some leftover from the last barbecue at my crib. Fuck all that, though. I wanna know what the fuck happened to the lil homies. Did you see the shit go down?"

"Man, it happened damn near right in front of me. I was choppin' it up with the connect when some niggas pulled up in a minivan. Niggas had a choppa. Aired the lil homies out."

"Yeah?" There was a dramatic pause before Kevin continued. "Damn, unc. The fuck? Why they didn't go to the Dreezy show with everybody else?"

"Fuck if I know."

"That shit don't make no sense. Damn...I heard one of the niggas got arrested last night. I think they say his dumb ass posted somethin' on Twitter about the shooting. That's what got him ran up."

"Which one was it?"

"Some nigga named Big Jay. I never met the lil nigga before but Tara said I know him. Said he used to fuck with some chick who lived down the street from us on Trumbull."

"Yeah, ol' girl said it was Big Jay and Darren. Said she saw em at the store or something,right before they came through."

"Lil Darren? Off 13th?"

"I don't know. I'm guessing that's where he's from. Never met the lil nigga." Juice shook his head. Last night's shooting was still fresh in his mind.

He ended the call and went to the living room sofa to watch Sportscenter and check out what was going on on Facebook until Kevin and Tara arrived.

The first dozen or so posts on his news feed were mostly related to the murders of Lil Dave and Head. Some were well wishes and prayers for their families, while others were rants about how the gun violence needed to stop. Juice remembered that in his smartphone's photo gallery he had a two-month-old picture of himself standing with Head, Lil Dave, and about fifteen more North Lawndale residents in front of Kev's house on 15th and Homan Avenue. He uploaded the photo to Facebook along with a praying emoji and the caption: 'Rest up, young bulls. #PrayForMyCity '

As expected, numerous likes and comments followed. Just about everyone in the North Lawndale neighborhood had known Lil Dave and Head, and most of the hood was on Juice's friends list.

He was liking the comments when his daughters, Dawn and Shawnna, came stomping down the stairs looking incredibly tired and grumpy.

Juice turned to them and smiled. The girls were always so caught up in the latest fashion trends that he hardly ever saw them without their hair and makeup done, so it was refreshing to see them trudging barefoot down the stairs in their pajama pants and shirts, wearing no makeupor fake eyelashes, their heads wrapped in matching silk Gucci headscarves. They were identical twins (aside from the fact that Dawn had hazel eyes, whereas Shawnna's were gray), and God were they beautiful. As much as Juice hated to admit it, he knew that his daughters were what men in the streets often referred to as "bad bitches". They were thick like their mother and as pretty as can be. Two prominent Chicago recording artists had recently featured them as lead models in their music videos. All the men in North Lawndale regarded them as neighborhood sexsymbols.

Juice absolutely hated it.

Shakela's nose wasn't her only superpower. She also had bionic ears, or at least that's howJuice and the kids saw it.

"Who is that coming down the stairs?" she shouted from the kitchen. "Dawn? Shawnna? Iknow it's one of you."

Shawnna groaned and rolled her eyes. "What do you want, Ma?" she muttered sleepily asshe and Dawn plopped down on either side of Juice and rested their faces on his shoulders.

"Y'all better get in here and help me with this food," Shakela shouted back.

Another groan from Shawnna. She and Dawn had stayed up with Shakela drinking wine (it was the only alcoholic beverage their mother allowed them to consume) and watching recorded episodes of Scandal they'd missed this past week.

Shawnna requested a moment's rest. She was dead tired. Her eyes were already shut.

"Daddy," Dawn said, pulling back to look Juice in the eye, "can you get me some rims for my car? Please?"

Juice looked at her like she was crazy. Dawn's car — a red, new model Dodge Charger that Juice and Shakela had given her as an eighteenth birthday present back in March — wasperfectly fine with the factory rims it had on it.

"You don't need no rims," Juice said, rubbing her arm and planting a kiss on her forehead. "Ialready spoil you enough as it is. And you see how niggas been robbing and killing out here. You don't wanna be riding around with expensive rims on your car. That's asking for trouble."

"That's bull, Daddy, and you know it.""No, it ain't."

"Well, if it ain't," Dawn challenged, "then why did you get twenty-sixes put on thatCadillac? Why did you have those sixes put on Mama's truck? It ain't adding up."

"Add up your own money for some rims. That's what you do." Juice grinned widely. Heslapped the girls on their arms and told them to go help their mother prepare the food.

Dawn sucked her teeth as she and Shawnna got up. "You need to be making Junior's lazy butt get up and help cook," she mumbled.

Juice chuckled once and went back to watching Sportscenter. He wasn't about to wake uphis son, Lee Wilkins, Jr. Junior was the star quarterback at Collins Academy High School. With the hours upon hours of practicing and traveling he endured with his teammates, he needed all the sleep he could get. The girls often complained that Juice was too soft on Junior, that Junior got away with everything and they got away with nothing, that Juice loved Junior more than he loved them.

They could not have been farther from the truth.

Juice was proud of all three of his children — for the most part. He wasn't too happy about Shawnna letting her ex-boyfriend crash the car (a 2016 Charger like Dawn's) he'd gotten her for her eighteenth birthday, and he wasn't too pleased that Shawnna had shot at some girl a few weeks ago over the same guy who destroyed her car, but other than that he was happy with the kids. They were all on the right track career-wise. Junior was looking forward to playing footballprofessionally. The twins had two more weeks of school to finish before they could become licensed cosmetologists and start making money doing hair, which is what they loved to do.

The only person who didn't have a career plan was the man of the house. Juice was a drug- dealer, always had been and probably always would be. His wife didn't understand his love for the fast money, but she never complained. Like the kids, she was more than happy to reap the benefits of his hustle. There were days when Juice would come home with $10,000 in cash. Sure, there were the occasional losses and arrests, but to Juice it was worth it. He had a long list of drug-related felonies on his record dating back to the early nineties; in his mind, his only way of having a good, high-paying job was to be a dope boy.

Five minutes passed before Kev and Tara walked in with the dishes of spaghetti and potato salad. Juice gave Tara a hug and then went out to the front porch with Kev to talk business.

Of all the TVL gang members Juice associated himself with, Kev was the realest. He trustedKev more than he trusted anyone else. Kev was a pretty boy to the ladies and a wise youngleader of the Vice Lord gang.

Kev's fitted cap was worn to the back and turned a little to the left. He wore a white T-shirt over blue jean True Religion shorts and white-and-blue Jordans. He lit up a Newport. Juice shouted for Shawnna to bring them two beers from the kitchen.

"Fucked up how they did the lil homies," Kev said, shaking his head in disbelief. "You already know how I carried Lil Dave. I'm fucked up over that. One of them niggas gotta get it for that shit."

Juice nodded his head as he lit his own cigarette and blew a puff of smoke at the sky.

"You know how dumb these lil niggas done got out here," Juice said. "We can't let that getin the way of the money. I just bought a whole slab. About to cook it up and dump it on y'all. That'll be a little over twenty-five thousand dollars to split between you and the lil homies. Just give me eleven hundred off each ounce."

Kev's somber disposition brightened instantly. Juice could almost see the numbers register inKev's eyes.

"Damn, and that shit gon' sell so fast. It's been a drought on hard for the last four or five days. I know a nigga that got the whole forty racks for a brick right now. Ain't nobody got nosoft or hard out our way. That'll be gone in a week tops. I guarantee it won't last no more than a week."

Juice became thoughtful. Rolling the butt of his cigarette between thumb and forefinger, he tried to decide whether or not he would sell the second kilo whole or break it down like the first one. Selling it whole wouldn't hurt him at all, but it would mean less money for him and hiscrew, and right now he needed every dollar he could get. He had to have the cash ready for the beauty salon he was going to get for the twins, plus the $15,000 down payment on the larger suburban home he and Shakela wanted to move into by Christmas. As of now they had a combined total of $35,000 in the bank, most of which was his. He also had over $22,000 in cash hidden away at his mom's house. The rest of his dirty money had gone to bills and his family's daily living expenses.

"Apple dropped off that strap at my spot a lil bit ago," Kev said as Shawnna finally deliveredthe beers. "I got it in the car. Ain't no telling when we gon' need to use that muhfucka. I just sent some lil niggas over there to see if they can find the nigga Darren. We might fuck around and getdragged into the shit ourselves."

"Nah." Juice shook his head and cracked open the beer. "We ain't young and dumb, nephew.

We'll stay out the way and get this money. Let the lil soldiers ride for us."

Little did either of them know, they would be needing their guns a lot sooner than they thought.

Chapter 5

There were fifteen of them, all members of the New Breeds street gang, all armed teenagers with red eyes and icy cold demeanors. About half of them had dreadlocks and thirty-round clips in their pistols. Most of them had been up all night. Many were still geeked up over a fight they'd had with some TVLs at Red Diamond at around three o'clock this morning.

One of those dread heads was Darren.

They were congregating in the alleyway behind the apartment building on 13th and Sawyer. The seven cars lined up in the alleyway belonged to them. The five girls they had with them were also members of the gang, though the vast majority of the gang's criminal activities were carried out by its male members. Drugs were being sold at one end of the alley: heroin, Molly, and Kush.

It was a quarter past ten in the morning. Some of the guys were talking about Big Jay's arrest. Apparently, Big Jay had sent out an incriminating tweet on Twitter regarding the shooting. It wasn't surprising that he'd done it — nowadays, social media was the way a lot of young gang members addressed their beefs — but Darren had expected Big Jay to play it smarterthan that. The tweet read: 'Nother Opp Down on Drake!!! How Dat Choppa Feel Lil Dave??!!' Big Jay had deleted it but not before it was retweeted more than two hundred times. Shaila had somehow managed to get a screenshot of the tweet and showed it to Darren.

"You all right?" Shaila asked. She and Darren were leaning back against the side of an old school Oldsmobile on large chrome rims.

He nodded. "I'm good. Shit, I ain't really got a choice. We gotta stay strong through this shit.Never break. Never fold." Darren's eyes kept sweeping to the right and to the left and back to theright again.

"You need to get out here and get some money," Shaila said as she dug a pinkie fingernail into a sandwich bag of coke and sniffed. "You know it's over for him, right? Big Jay ain't cominghome. Ever. He fucked up royally this time. I mean, how dumb can you get? I know if I"

"He'll be home. You tweakin'." Darren gritted his teeth. He didn't like hearing negative things about his fellow gang members. He looked at them like brothers. Big Jay was like family to him. "And I got some money," he added.

It wasn't exactly a lie. He had ninety dollars and some change on him now. It wasn't much, but it was more than he was used to having in his pocket.

Darren could not stop glancing around. It was early in the day, certainly much too early to be worried about retaliation, but then again you never knew. It had been daytime when Rocky, one of Darren's best friends since elementary school, was shot and killed just two blocks over a few weeks ago. It had also been daytime when Darren's father was murdered in the Austin neighborhood two years back. There were really no safe times to be outside in any Chicago ghetto when the gangs were at war.

Taking a long pull from his cigarette, he took off walking up the alleyway. He had to piss.

He looked back and saw that Shaila was trailing along behind him.

"You ain't gotta follow me. I ain't about to do nothing but take a piss," Darren said.

"So? I can't come with you? What you taking, a top-secret piss? A G-13 Classified piss?""Keep talkin' and I'ma piss on you," Darren threatened jokingly.

He let loose a stream of pee on the side of someone's garage while puffing his cigarette and reading a muddied McDonald's receipt that was stuck against the side of an empty cup from the same restaurant.

Darren didn't know the people whose garage he was pissing on. All he knew was that they were a good, church-going family of five who rarely ventured outside unless it was to walk downthe street to church. None of the gang members ever bothered them. The man of the house was a pastor who had a clean-ass Jaguar that Darren and the gang often plotted on stealing, but no one ever touched it. Darren knew it was the family's devotion to the church that kept them safe from harm. Sure, there were loners who still might try something one day, but not likely. The gang usually committed crimes against other criminals. Plus, the pastor had three beautiful teenage daughters that all the guys loved to see.

The pastor's family was safe; it was Darren who needed a prayer.

Shaila sucked her teeth and put her hands on her hips. "Before I forget, you need to explain what's going on between you and that hoe who used to work at the Taco Bell down the street. My baby cousin's girlfriend said she was at some party the other night and saw you smiling all in thatbitch's face. What's up with that? I mean, you do know her twin sister shot at me over a nigga that's fucking like three other thot bitches."

"Shut up." Darren turned to face her, shaking the last drops of urine from the head of his phallus and biting down on his dry bottom lip. "Suck on this muhfucka for me. Ain't nobody gon'see us."

"You ain't about to have me all out here like some lil thot hoe," Shaila said, but she was moving toward him with an outstretched hand, smiling a devilishly pretty smile. She looked backto make sure they were alone before she squatted down on her haunches and took his dick in her mouth.

It took less than a minute for Darren to become fully erect. Shaila's juicy, full lips pushedand pulled on his engorged pole. He put a hand on her shoulder and urged her to continue by easing his hips forward.

Darren's back was to the pastor's house; Shaila's back was to the alleyway. She didn't notice it when Tocka, one of her female friends, stuck a smartphone around the corner of the garage,but she heard the friend shout, "Ooh, bitch, you finna be on World Star for this!"

Darren laughed, and Shaila seemed to gather more energy as she began to suck him faster, taking his entire length down her throat.

Five minutes later he came in her mouth. She sucked until the last drops of cum were out of him, then opened her mouth and showed it to him before turning and spitting it out right on topof the McDonald's receipt.

Shaila was rising to her feet when the bullets started flying.

Three guys who Darren knew from school as members of the TVLs came running into the alleyway firing at Darren's gang. One of them had a Tec 9, and the other two had handguns with extended magazines. Their eyes were set on the crowd of New Breeds; Darren, Shaila, andTocka could see them, but the shooters weren't looking their way.

Darren was glad that Shaila and Tocka had enough sense not to scream. Instead, the twogirls ran into the pastor's backyard, with Darren close behind them. He ducked low behind the garage, took the 9-millimeter Ruger pistol off his hip, and breathed steadily for a few seconds.

Then he stuck his head around the corner of the garage, aimed his gun at the head of one of the enemies, and started pulling the trigger.

The guy went down instantly and didn't move again. Darren kept firing, watching as the bullets knocked blood and puffs of dirt up from the ground around the guy's body. He didn't stop shooting until the guy's skull opened up and released its clumpy brain matter.

The other two shooters sprinted away, and seconds later the sound of screeching tires signaled their departure.

The Vice Lords had just changed the score.

Darren and Shaila rejoined the crowd and found two of the New Breed gang members dead in the alleyway. Seven others were wounded, including three girls. It was ironic that the wounded girls were quiet, while the unharmed girls were screaming their lungs out for help. One girl kept screaming, "Somebody call the police! Somebody call nine-one-one!"

Ronnie, a Breed who'd been born and raised here on Sawyer, had a gunshot wound to the abdomen and another to his right knee. Darren helped him into the backseat of Shaila's ten-year- old Buick. Then he reclined in the passenger seat as Shaila sped off to the hospital.

Chapter 6

Shawnna Wilkins was the wild card in the Wilkins household; there was no questioning it. Her twin sister was daddy's little angel, while she herself could essentially be described as daddy's little demon. Over the years she'd been suspended from school on numerous occasions, arrested twice for brawling with girls over boys, and she was known for carrying a gun that everyone knew she was not afraid to use.

She absolutely detested the fact that Dawn had a car and she didn't. It was bullshit. Daddy could have easily bought her a new whip after Jacoby, her ex-boyfriend, had crashed her Charger. It wasn't like Kobe had been drunk-driving; he had actually been on the way to pick her up from Paul Mitchell hair school when a minivan full of rival gang members pulled up alongside the car and opened fire. Kobe had taken two bullets to the forearm as he sped away, and he ended up crashing into another car at the Marathon gas station on Laramie and Division.

Shawnna was gritting her teeth as Dawn continued to search the internet for the perfect set of rims. They were in the backyard, dressed in plain white crop tops and identical, snug-fitting white denim shorts that had the four boys who lived across the alley staring out the window at them.

Mama's orders were to set up their two picnic tables for the barbecue, but Shawnna was the only one working, which made her clench her teeth even tighter. The only reason Shawnna wasn't complaining was because Dawn always let her drive the car, and driving it while it was on a huge set of rims was a surefire way to infuriate her haters.

Shawnna's number-one hater was the girl Kobe had cheated on her with, the girl she'd recently shot at.

"I swear," Shawnna said as she draped a checkered tablecloth over one of the picnic tables, "if Daddy get you those rims he gotta get me another car. I don't care if it's a few years old. I just need some wheels. I can't take this shit."

"You can get a car if you want one. You know who to ask. That nigga Bankroll Reese will buy you a car today, bitch. And you know it."

Shawnna rolled her eyes at the suggestion. Bankroll Reese was a multimillionaire who'd inherited a large fortune and a slew of nightclubs from his now deceased father. Shawnna and Dawn's best friend Myesha was a dancer at one of Bankroll Reese's strip clubs. Every time the twins showed up to support Myesha he tried to get them to leave with him. He'd offered them cash for sex more than once. He'd offered them jobs at the club, both as dancers and as bottle girls. Shawnna had already thought to ask Reese for some money, but judging from the recently uploaded photos on his Instagram account he was currently vacationing with a swimsuit model atthe Sandals resort in Montego Bay, Jamaica.

Unbeknownst to Bankroll Reese, he was just as irresistible to Shawnna as she was to him. Even more so, really, since he was a millionaire and they were basically poor. Shawnna followed his social media accounts religiously. She knew his net worth ($52 million according to celebritynetworth.com's latest estimate); she knew his height and weight (6'2", 175 lbs.); she knew that he owned seven nightclubs and two strip clubs and that one of the girls from Love and Hip Hop New York was trying to pin a pregnancy on him.

The only thing holding Shawnna back from approaching Bankroll Reese was Daddy.

Cup, Bankroll Reese's deceased father, had been Juice's closest friend. Last summer he was shot and killed by some crazy Mexican lady inside The Visionary Lounge, his most popular Chicago nightclub. Since then Bankroll Reese had taken over his father's many companies. Everybody in the streets knew it.

"I actually was already thinking about reaching out to Reese," Shawnna said. "You might beright. He's smart, handsome, local."

"Better off fucking with him than with Kobe's bum ass. You out here fighting over a nigga that ain't even got a car when you can be laid up with a nigga that got a Lamborghini. Hoe, you trippin'."

Shawnna shrugged. "Money ain't everything. I actually loved that nigga Kobe. You of all people know all the shit we went through. If you saw him nine times out of ten me and you were with him, and vice versa. That was really love. You can't buy that."

Dawn made a "pshh" sound with her lips. "Love ain't on shit. Get on that money train and watch how many niggas fall in love with your ass. Get with him and poke a hole in the condom like Myesha told us to do when we were with those rappers that night. Get that good childsupport money out his rich ass. Make me an auntie. I'll gladly be the rich baby's auntie. Maybe when he grows up he'll buy auntie a million-dollar mansion."

Shawnna gave her twin a sideways stare. "Well, why don't you fuck the nigga? Since you

got this grand scheme all planned out. You look just like me; it ain't like he'll know thedifference."

"Yeah, but I'm not a whore like you." Dawn said it very nonchalantly and with a growing smirk.

"Tell that to somebody who doesn't know you." Shawnna put emphasis on the 'doesn't'. "Be honest with yourself. Most of the time if I'm getting dicked down, you're somewhere in the same room getting the same treatment. Did you forget about prom night? You fucked two guys atonce. I've never done that. That makes you the whore."

It was Shawnna's turn to smirk, but the verbal victory was short lived.

Dawn's fingers skated down the screen of her smartphone to the contacts icon. She touched it and scrolled down to the name Big Bank. The name had money bag emojis on both sides of it. She touched the name, turned on the speakerphone, and handed over the phone to her sister.

Shawnna gasped at the sound of the phone ringing. "Is this...?" she murmured weakly.Dawn only nodded.

The next few seconds were like an eternity to Shawnna, and when Bankroll Reese answered she sucked in another gasp.

"Hello?" Reese's voice sounded tired and husky, almost hoarse.

"I'm so sorry to bother you while you're out of the country," Shawnna said as she reachedout and pinched Dawn on the shoulder. "This is Shawnna, one of the twins. Um...I don't wanna sugar-coat what I'm about to say to you so I'll just say it. I'm single and my sister just called you out the blue to hook us up. You're always trying to get at us sooooo...are you—"

"Actually, I'm back in Chicago," Bankroll Reese said, cutting her off. "We just toucheddown at O'Hare like thirty minutes ago. Where y'all at?"

"At our parents' house on Central Park. We're having a barbecue."

"Bet, I'm on my way. Gotta talk to your pops anyway. Don't know why he ain't hit my line, Igave him my number when he first got out the joint."

Shawnna's expression twisted in discontent. The number-one thing she loved about herfather was the wisdom she gained from the family discussions he often had with them, but what she didn't like was her father talking to one of her potential lovers. That was a bit much.

"Don't worry," Reese added, "I'll keep what's between us between us. I'm definitely trying to

see where this little adventure gets me. I hope it's in bed with bo—" He paused midsentence, andShawnna spoke before he could continue.

"You know my sis ain't shit like me. She got a man. And we don't share men. Well, wehaven't done it before. I suggested it once but she was all in love with the nigga."

Reese laughed at this. "See y'all in a couple minutes," he said, and then hung up.

Chapter 7

Reese's dazzling smile spoke volumes about his deep-seated feelings for the Wilkins twins. He took off his white-framed Louis Vuitton sunglasses and looked out his window at the passingscenery.

2 Chains had not been the only black man going online in search of the Bentley SUV's arrival. Reese had placed a pre-order for the Bentley Bentayga long before most American millionaires had even heard of it. The quarter-million-dollar "Bentley truck" was custom painted black and gold and it had all the available add-ons, including a massive set of 24 karat gold 28- inch Forgiato rims.

Seated in the backseat behind his driver, Reese was feeling amazing. He had just spent the weekend at a couples resort in Jamaica, making love to a flawless, caramel-complected black girl he'd met in New York City a while back, smoking huge blunts of the very best Kush anddrinking cognac like a fish drinks water.

He was dressed in all white: a thin silk Versace shirt over Balmain jeans and Christian Louboutin sneakers. The baguette-cut diamond decorated Chopard L.U.C Tourbillon watch on his right wrist was worth more than the Bentley SUV. The necklace he was wearing had large white diamonds just like the two bracelets on his left wrist. The backs of his iPhone 6S smartphones were also white. His throat was sore from smoking Kush and turning up allweekend with his two closest friends — Chubb and Suwu — who also doubled as his bodyguards.

Chubb was driving the Bentayga like a madman, while Suwu sat next to him eating anItalian beef sandwich. Unlike Reese, the two armed bodyguards were large in size and heavyset. They were paid $10,000-a-month to travel everywhere with Reese.

"Who was that on the phone?" Chubb asked. He kept glancing over at Suwu's sandwich."The twins," Reese said.

"Them OTF niggas?"

"Nah. The girl twins. The bad bitches. Juice's daughters."

"Oh, shit. Damn. Man, those two bad lil muhfuckas make my heart stop every time I see em. Bitches just don't get no prettier than them. You know your pops used to be like this with Juice." Chubb crossed his index and middle fingers. "You know how close I was to Cup. I'm telling you,he looked at Juice just like he looked at me."

"On everything I love," Suwu said with a mouthful of sandwich, "I honestly think Shawnna and Dawn are the baddest bitches in the hood."

"Nigga, gimme some of that sandwich," Chubb said, reaching for it.

"You just ate two of em and I didn't say shit," Suwu countered, moving his meal out of Chubb's reach. "Lemme eat mine in peace."

"Nigga, you gon' rest in peace if you don't gimme some of—"

"Man," Reese cut in, "will you two wide backed, uh, Rick Ross built ass niggas please stoparguing over that sandwich. Chubb, yo' fat ass need to go on a diet."

Chubb turned the rearview mirror so he could look Bankroll Reese right in the eyes. He gavethe young millionaire an icy stare that made both Reese and Suwu crack up laughing.

When the laughter subsided Suwu said, "Nah, but for real though, ol' girl n'em bad. Whatthey on?"

Reese's smile returned. "Shawnna wanna fuck with the kid.""I'd be trying to get both of em," Suwu said.

"Think I ain't?" Reese had wanted to fuck the Wilkins twins ever since he first laid eyes on them two years ago. Then they were just sixteen years old, but now they were grown. Now they were grown and sexy and thick and ready for the taking.

He told Chubb to head over to Juice's place, then deleted a text message from Jalisa, the girl who'd been with him in Jamaica. He'd sent her home to New York on a first-class flight with promises to contact her later in the day. In all honesty he knew that he would never contact her again. He hated that he'd given her his phone number in the first place. Jalisa was just another freak with a flawless body. There were tens of thousands more just like her all across the globe. Reese was used to seeing them. He was used to having sex with them and then ditching them likeused condoms.

Which is why he wasn't sure what to do about the twins.

He couldn't treat them like he treated other women. No, not the daughters of the man who'dbeen his father's best friend. But not pursuing them wasn't an option. There was just one other pair of sisters from the North Lawndale neighborhood that Reese was so attracted to that he would pay for a night with them. The Lyon sisters — Tamera and Tirzah — were pretty-faced and thick just like the Wilkins twins, but they were married now. He'd tried to get with Tirzah, promising himself that he would for the first time attempt to be in a monogamous relationship, but Tirzah turned him down and got married to Jah, a guy Reese had gone to school with in elementary. Aside from Tamera and Tirzah, Shawnna and Dawn were his biggest crushes.

As if reading Reese's mind, Chubb said, "One of these days you gon' have to settle down and live like a grown man is supposed to live, and I think one of the twins would be perfect for you. Put a baby in one of them sexy muhfuckas. I know I would if I had the chance. You know they want you. You got bread like Bulletface."

"I ain't got that much money." Reese laughed at the comparison. Blake "Bulletface" King was a billionaire, the wealthiest rapper in all of Hip-Hop, and he was married to the richest woman in the world.

"Shit," Suwu said, "like Gucci said in that "Birdman" song, 'I ain't got money like Birdman but in East Atlanta I'm Birdman'. You know the song. You might not have money like Bulletface but in Chiraq you Bulletface, nigga. You got more bread than any—"

"Stop that shit, bruh. I might have money but I had to lose my daddy to get this shit. I'll give all this shit up to bring him back."

Chubb and Suwu got quiet. Reese swallowed a two-milligram Xanax pill and took a deep breath, then picked up his double stacked Styrofoam cups full of Fanta soda and purple Actavis Prometh with Codeine on ice from the cup holder next to his seat. As much as he hated to admit it, Reese did view himself as the closest thing his neighborhood had to rappers like Gucci Mane and Bulletface. It was partly the reason why he drank so much Lean and smoked Kush all day. It was the reason he always hit up strip clubs in every city he visited to throw at least $5,000 at the twerking dancers, why he had a dozen foreign cars and trucks in the driveway of his Burr Ridge mansion. He wanted to put on for Holy City (an area of the North Lawndale neighborhood where the Vice Lord gang originated). He wanted to be a rich street nigga like his father had been, only without dabbling in the drug trade.

He gazed out his window as they entered the North Lawndale neighborhood and headed down 16th Street. As always he was excited to be back in the hood. People started shouting at theBentley as it passed them: a group of teenage girls on Kedzie; three older women walking out of the convenience store on Sawyer; four cars full of gang members and women that were driving past.

The shouts were welcoming; Reese lowered his window and shouted back. He loved his neighborhood, though he adamantly refused to be drawn in to the drug dealing and other formsof crime that plagued the area. He often gave money to old friends of his, knowing what it wouldbe used for, but he never dealt with the drugs. Not unless it was some Kush or pills or Actavis hewas getting for himself. His father had lost his life to the dope game, along with countless other Lawndale residents. Reese was determined not to join the statistics.

There was only one man Reese was willing to assist in buying drugs, and so far that man hadturned him down every time he offered a helping hand.

That man was named Lee “Juice” Wilkins.

Chapter 8

"Daddy, you ain't gon' believe who I just got off the phone with," Shawnna said fromoutside the locked bedroom door.

Juice flicked his eyes at the door and then returned to what he was doing, which was twiddling his tongue across his wife's clitoris while she rubbed his bald head and winded herwide hips in tune with the Chris Brown song that was blaring from her stereo system.

"Daddy!" Shawnna repeated. "Can y'all even hear me over that loud ass music?"

Reluctantly, Juice lifted his head. It was difficult to do with Shakela's fingers clamped to his skull.

"I hear you, Shawnna. Give us a minute," he said, loud enough to eclipse the music.

"Okay, well, hurry up. I just talked to Bankroll Reese. He's on the way over, said he needs totalk to you. And Kev said the food's about ready to eat. We got people showing up. Tanjra and Anissa just got here with their kids. Rell and Jah and their wives. Y'all need to come on. Everybody's ready to eat."

Juice had left Kevin in charge of the barbecue while he and Shakela ventured off to the bedroom for a half hour or so of quality time.

He went back to licking and listening to Shakela's gentle moans. In the back of his mind he thought of Bankroll Reese and wondered why the young millionaire was coming to the barbecue. Juice had loved Reese's father like his own blood, but he like being around Reese. The kid was filthy rich. Juice didn't like that kind of attention, and he didn't want Reese trying to help him out financially. He'd never been the type to follow up behind someone for money and popularity. He'd hated seeing it happen in prison, so much so that he absolutely refused to hang around anyone but family now.

But there was a catch-22 situation with Reese, and it involved Kevin.

Leonard Wilkins, Juice's older brother who was now serving a thirty-year prison sentence in Stateville Correctional Center, was

Kevin's father. Kevin's mother, however, had a daughter by another man, and that daughter — Kevin's sister, Rose — was Reese's mother. So, Kevin was Juice's nephew, and Bankroll Reese was Kevin's nephew, which meant that Juice and Reese weren't related but were practically family. A lot of times when Juice phoned Kevin he heard Reese in the background. When Kevin's SUV broke down a few weeks agoReese had wired him the money to fix it. Sometimes when Juice and Kev would go out for a night on the town, Kev would pull up in Reese's black Lamborghini Gallardo. There had been several times when Juice ran out of drugs to distribute and Kev took up the slack by using cash he'd gotten from Reese to get more product.

None of that mattered right now. Right now it was all about pleasing Shakela. She was a beautiful, loyal black queen, and she deserved to be pleased when she needed it.

Her juices were as sweet as honey. Juice liked to stick his tongue inside of her when she orgasmed. He craved the taste of her juicy nookie more than he did a cold beer on a hot sunny day like today.

He caressed Shakela's thick thighs and continued to work his tongue on her until she came a moment later.

He rose to his knees and whipped out the love stick, ready to plunge into her and do some damage.

"Nuh uh." Shakela rolled out of bed and started getting dressed. "We have company. We'll get back to this later. And besides, I smelled perfume on you when you walked in earlier. Don't think you're off the hook that easily. I'm gonna find out whose makeup that was on your shirt. If you fucked that bitch you're gonna have hell to pay."

Chapter 9

Bankroll Reese's obnoxiously expensive Bentley SUV was just pulling up next to the house when Juice and Shakela walked out onto the back porch.

Several more family members and their children had arrived since Shawnna's announcement, some with food and liquor to add to the festivities, others with empty hands. Juice didn't mind the freeloaders. There would be times when the tables were turned. All that mattered was that they were together and enjoying themselves on this warm 4th of July holiday.

Juice hugged and greeted his family and friends with open arms before taking over the grill. Kev stood there with him, making plates and smoking a cigarette. There was an odd expression on Kev's face. He was waiting to tell Juice something; Juice could tell.

"Juice, what it is, unc?" Reese said as he walked up with two large guys Juice had gone to school with named Chubb and Suwu.

Juice and Chubb were close friends. He also knew Suwu well. They were all from right here in the same neighborhood, and had spent innumerable days and nights drinking and smoking together.

Shaking Reese's hand, Juice took a second to admire the young man's jewelry and clothing. Reese looked a lot like his father, only he was a lot more flashy. Juice guessed that the purple iced beverage in Reese's Styrofoam cups was Lean. He also guessed that, behind the dark lenses of the designer sunglasses, Reese's eyes were bloodshot.

"I see you, lil nigga." Juice chuckled. "Ball one time for your pops. I know he gotta be proudof you."

"Man, why you ain't hit my phone?" Reese reached over to Suwu and grabbed his smartphone. "What's your number?"

Juice let loose another chuckle, but he gave Reese his number.

"I don't be calling niggas like that," Juice said. "Not unless it's about some money.""It is about some money."

"I don't want your money, Reese. Trust me, I make enough by myself. More than enough."

Chubb said, "Juice, ain't nothing wrong with getting help from your own people. I ain't gon' lie to you, if it wasn't for the job Reese gave me, I'd be asking him for some help my-damn-self. It's hard out here. Lil homie got us eating like Cup had us eating."

"And all you gotta do," Reese said, sipping from his Styrofoam, "is take a seat at the table and eat with us. It's as simple as that. I'll make sure you and your family are well taken care of. I'll get you out of that lil Cadillac and put you in something foreign. I'll do all that, and give you what you really need."

"You ain't got what I really need. Only muhfucka that got what I need just took a trip to Mexico," Juice countered. He would have said more had his mother not approached him for a plate at that very moment.

Sheryl was closing in on sixty years of age. She had a full head of gray hair and crow's feet in the corners of her eyes. Her smile seemed permanent.

"How you been doing, Lee?" she asked as Reese and his bodyguards excused themselves and headed over to one of the picnic tables. Kev went with them.

"I'm good, Ma." Juice hugged Sheryl for the second time and planted a firm kiss on her cheek. "Just getting this money together for the girls' hair salon. You know how much they love hair. It's the dumbest thing in the world to me but hey, whatever floats their boat."

"Girls love hair, Lee. Look how Shawnna got me lookin'." Sheryl patted her neatly done hair. Shawnna had given her a nice little bob the other night. Mama loved getting her hair done.

"Ma, you always look good."

"I know. Where you think y'all gotcha looks from?" She laughed heartily as Juice and Shakela made her two heaping plates of baked spaghetti with cheese, chicken breasts, baked beans, potato salad, macaroni and cheese, and collard greens.

As he carried Mama's plate to the table he noticed that Dawn and Shawnna were sitting across from Reese at the other table.

Juice didn't like the ear-to-ear smiles his daughters were displaying.

He knew how they looked when they saw a boy they liked. There was a glow to their faces,a noticeable sparkle in their eyes.

It didn't help that the twins had inherited the beauty and thickness their mother possessed. Sometimes — particularly at times like this — Juice wished his daughters were ugly.

Luckily, Rell and Jah's wives were meatier than the twins. Tamera and Tirzah were standing next to the same table Reese and the twins were seated at, dressed in revealing mini dresses and red-bottomed Louboutin heels. (Juice knew that the heels were Louboutin; he'd bought the twins Christian Louboutin heels for their high school prom). Chubb and Suwu's eyes were unwaveringly glued to Tirzah and Tamera, and Juice didn't blame them for looking.

Rell and Jah were talking to Kev. They were blood brothers from off 13th and Avers, and they too were TVLs. After their father's death they'd gotten a million dollars each and a few houses their father had been renting out. The hood viewed them as success stories now. Rell and Jah had snow white Mercedes Benz S550s, both of which were parked at the curb behind Reese'sluxury SUV.

"Baby," Shakela said to Juice, "go and see what's going on with Kev. Tara said somebody else done got killed."

"Somebody else?" Juice knitted his brows, then turned and walked over to where Kev and the guys were standing.

"Man, unc," Kev said, "the lil niggas I sent to take care of that situation got hit up, too. Lil Jock got whacked. I guess they killed two of the Breeds but them niggas shot back and hit Jock. Mark got hit in the leg, but him and K.T. got away."

"Y'all need me back out there," Jah said. He was a hothead, probably the most trigger-happy member of the gang. Everyone knew he had dropped numerous bodies in the hood. He was skinny and dark-skinned and as quick-tempered as can be. "Lucky I got some money now. I'd be over there on Sawyer whackin' everything, on Neal."

"Nah," said Rell. He was muscular, brown-complected like Juice, and more level-headed than his younger brother. "Somebody needs to squash that shit before it gets too out of hand. It's already so bad that a nigga can't even sit on the porch without gettin' shot at. That shit ain't cool. When I was out here hustlin' we only got into shootouts over turf and money. Now, it's gettin' to where these young niggas are shootin' just 'cause they see a nigga that ain't in the same gang, or 'cause their guy got into a fight and lost. Shit, they're barely even fighting. It's all gunfire."

Juice shook his head in disbelief. Lil Jock was one of Juice's favorite youngsters. Jock was always ready to fight, always willing to protect the hood from the enemies that were picking off his friends one by one. Jock had the kind of personality that no one could dislike.

The saddest part about it was that Jock was only fifteen.

"Damn," Juice muttered. He made a mental note to fix Jock's mother a plate.

As the barbecue went on, Juice noticed that the guys were more watchful than usual. They kept looking around, eyeing every vehicle that passed. Kev and his wife sat at the table with Reese to eat.

Juice ate while having smalltalk with Mama and Kela about the kids. Junior didn't join them until Tommy, one of his football teammates, arrived a half hour later.

Reese offered to pay $100 for the food he and his bodyguards consumed but Juice turned down the cash, so Reese slipped one bank-new bill out of a fresh ten-thousand-dollar packet of hundreds and gave the crisp Benjamin Franklin to Shawnna, who hastily tucked it away in her Michael Kors bag. Juice clenched his teeth together when Dawn stuck out her hand and got a Benjamin for herself.

"Our girls are grown, Juice," Shakela said, noticing his tight expression.

Juice nodded and said, "I know," but the mask of discontent did not leave his face...until Shakela's best friend pulled up to the house a few minutes later.

Shakela's best friend's name was Carol.

Carol's daughter was Chandra, and Chandra was in the car with Carol.

Chapter 10

After dropping off Ronnie at the hospital, Darren and Shaila returned home to 13th and Sawyer.

There were police officers and CPD vehicles everywhere, and the alley where the shooting took place was blocked off with yellow crime scene tape.

There was still blood in the alleyway, but the dead bodies were gone. So were the gang members. In fact, there were no residents outside, only policemen and two news crews — Fox 32and ABC 7.

Darren kept his eyes on his smartphone as he and Shaila entered the apartment building. An overpowering stench of urine hit him as they ascended the stairs. Shaila unlocked her front door and they went inside.

The dreary little apartment was just as dusty and unsanitary as it always was. There were roaches on the walls, and several more floating around in a bowl of milk on the coffee table. A thin layer of dust covered the screen of an ancient floor-model Zenith television across the room from a threadbare blue sofa. A dirty sock that looked like it too had been a victim of today's gun violence was dangling over the edge of the table.

"Lock that door," Darren said as he sat down on the beat-up old sofa and lit up a cigarette."No shit," Shaila retorted.

"Get me somethin' to drink."

"I got some Juicy Juice. And water. Which one you want?""Water. Put some ice in it."

"Ain't no ice."

"How in the fuck do you not have ice? You ain't got no ice trays?"

"Boy, you know I hardly even be here." It was the excuse Shaila always used. She went to the kitchen. "I'll let the cold water run for a minute."

"You do that."

"Oh, I'll tell you what I'm about to do. That bitch that shot at me the other day thinks it's cuteto get on Facebook and brag about the shit. I'm about to call my sister and we gon' pop out onthat hoe. I know where that bitch lives. And I'm bringing my gun, too. Let that bitch start shooting today. Bet I put an end to that shit."

Darren didn't care about any girl battles; he kicked his feet up on the coffee table, got on his phone, and dialed B Man's number.

"What up, bruh," B Man answered.

"Shit. Just got back from droppin' Ronnie off at the hospital. Where y'all at?"

"Ridin' around lookin' for somebody to shoot. We need to catch up with one of their top guys. Find out who the nigga is that's buying them all those fuckin' guns. They just killed two of our lil homies, bruh. Two. Cash Boy got hit twice. His sister got hit. We can't let that shit slide. I'm starting to think it's the nigga Reese that's giving them all those guns. It gotta be."

"Who, Bankroll Reese?"

"Yeah. You know he from over there. He got all that money. I heard he in town, too. My sister just saw his Bentley truck on 16th a lil while ago."

Darren paused to think it over. No, he thought, there was no way Reese could be involved with the ongoing war between the Travelers and the New Breeds. Reese wasn't the street type. He might act like a street nigga but really he was just a rich nigga from the block. He was too afraid of jail to be putting guns in the hands of known gang members. But then again, it could be Reese's money that was involved. Maybe it was Reese's financial assistance that had the Travelers so heavily armed. Darren had heard of times when Reese had given away thousands of dollars in cash to the guys on 15th and Trumbull, where his father was from. Reese's strip club was a block away from there.

Then Darren thought of another, more reasonable possibility.

Maybe it was Juice, the bald-headed chubby guy from 15th and Trumbull, who was responsible for the murders of Darren's friends. He knew that Juice was a high-ranking member of the TVLs, and that Juice's money was long (though nowhere near as long as Reese's money). It wasn't a farfetched assumption that Juice might be vicariously responsible for the attacks against Darren's guys. Everyone knew that Juice's dope was being pushed through most of North Lawndale's drug spots.

There was an easy way to find out.

"Let me make a few phone calls. I'll hit you right back," Darren said, and ended the call.

He dialed another number and put it on speakerphone as the phone rang. He was calling one of his fellow gang members who'd been in the house for the past few weeks, giving himself time to heal up after being shot in traffic.

When the call was answered, a female voice said, "Hello?""Who is this?" Darren asked.

"Nigga, you just called my nigga's phone. Don't you think I should be asking you that question?"

Darren laughed. "My bad. This is Darren. Can I talk to Kobe?"

Chapter 11

"Tell me why Kobe just texted me, sis. Talking about he's sorry and can I give him another chance. Hmm." Shawnna sucked her teeth and lifted the corner of her top lip in disgust.

She and Dawn were sitting on the stairs of their back porch, smoking blunts of potent high- grade marijuana with Chandra, Tara, and Rell and Jah's wives while The Weeknd's "The Hills" remix with Eminem and Nicki Minaj played loudly from the many speakers in Dawn's car, whichshe'd parked at the curb next to the backyard so that everyone could hear the music.

Bankroll Reese and his bodyguards had left over an hour ago with promises to return. Rell and Jah were at the picnic table playing a game of spades with Mama and Carol. Juice and Kev had left about five minutes after Bankroll Reese to take care of some business. Grandma Sheryl and the rest of the family were gone already.

Dawn gave her twin a skeptical look. "You better not text him back," she said. "The only nigga you need to be texting is Reese."

"Yeah, what she said," Tara said. "Nephew's a good nigga. He'll take good care of you. That nigga Kobe moved on to another bitch too damn fast. I heard he's all booed up with somestripper bitch over there on Drake."

"He is, too," Chandra said, nodding her head in agreement. "He's fucking Brianna. She lives right across the street from me."

"See what I mean? That nigga ain't shit." Dawn passed the blunt to Chandra; Tamera and Tirzah were smoking their blunt with Tara. "Reese, on the other hand, is a fine ass young nigga who wants you. He's the only person you should be focused on right now. You're my twin sister; you know I wouldn't tell you anything that wasn't good for you. I hope you're listening to me."

"Yeah, I'm listening. Professor. Fuck you asking me am I listening for?"The girls shared a laugh; Dawn flipped Shawnna the middle finger.

"We need to start hanging out together, y'all," Tara suggested. "This lil group right here is what's up. I already be chilling with Tam and Tirz damn near every day, and Kevin's always either over here with Juice or over Tamera's house with Rell and Jah. We're a perfect lil crew. Some real bitches, bad bitches, and we all get money and got niggas that get money. We're basically family."

"But we're far from being basic," Tamera added. "And we don't know this bitch right here."She looked at Chandra.

"Oh, I'm more family than y'all know," Chandra said with a smirk."What's that supposed to mean?" Tirzah asked.

"For real, though," Shawnna said.

Chandra shrugged. She was opening her mouth to respond when a raggedy old Buick came to a sudden stop in the middle of the street next to the Wilkins family's home.

Shawnna busted out laughing when she saw who the two girls were that jumped out of the Buick.

The driver was Shaila, the girl who'd sucked Kobe's dick in front of dozens of people at the strip club on 16th Street. Tara, who happened to be at the club that night, had recorded video of the incident and sent it to Shawnna's phone.

That same night, Shawnna drove Dawn's car over to the building where Shaila lived on Sawyer. She'd sat on the trunk of the Charger and waited impatiently for the bitch to show up. When Shaila pulled up and got out of the car, Shawnna took Kobe's 9 millimeter Glock out ofher purse and squeezed off several shots at Shaila, who immediately took off running in the opposite direction.

Apparently, Shaila was back for more, and this time she had a gun of her own, a black revolver with a short barrel. The girl with her was Evon, her sister.

"Yeah, bitch! What's up now? I see all that braggin' on Facebook! Step out here in this streetand take this ass whoopin' I got for you, whichever one of you bitches shot at me. I know it's Shawnna. Try to pull a gun out and see if I don't put a hole in yo' ass."

Shawnna stared thoughtfully at Shaila; the other girls on the stairs with her stood up, but neither of them spoke. Mama and Carol got up, too. So did Jah and Rell, both of whom drewtheir own pistols.

"You wanna fight me?" Shawnna stepped off the porch. "Put the gun down. We can fight.""Bitch," Jah shouted, "you better put that strap down 'fore I pop yo' dumb ass."

Shaila handed the gun to her sister, and Shawnna walked out into the street.

"Kick her mothafuckin ass, Shawnna," Mama said as she too headed out of the backyard.

The pistol in Evon's hand made Shawnna a bit nervous, but as soon as Evon put the gun in the waistline of her shorts Shawnna rushed forward and socked Shaila with a solid punch to the forehead.

The fight was underway.

Shawnna grabbed a handful of Shaila's shirt with one hand and swung with the other, punching Shaila several more times before Shaila could even get a single punch off.

She heard the girls cheering her on in the background. Her punches were connecting withharsh-sounding thuds.

"Beat that bitch's ass!" Tirzah shouted.

"Show her, sis," Dawn said. "Fight her like we fight Junior. Slam that hoe.""And bitch, if you pull out that gun..." Jah warned angrily.

Shaila was clumsy; she fell on her ass in the middle of the street, which was the absoluteworst thing to do when fighting a girl like Shawnna.

Shawnna sat on Shaila's chest and started punching with both hands. "You gorilla-facedbitch, I will fucking killed you," she said in between punches.

"Get off me!" Shaila screamed.

Evon said, "Let her up," but before she could get the whole word 'up' out Dawn and Tirzah were on her, punching her in the face and head, while Tamera stripped her of the pistol.

When Shawnna looked back and saw the girls stomping Evon out, she turned back to Shaila and slammed the back of the girl's head on the street until Shaila lost consciousness. Then shespit in Shaila's face, stood up, and delivered a vicious kick to Shaila's jaw that sent a tooth skittering across the street and a mist of blood into the air.

"Stupid ass bitch. Got me fucked up." She kicked Shaila in the side of the head and was about to do it again when Mama grabbed her and pulled her away.

"That's enough, Shawnna. She's out cold," Mama said.

Shawnna was upset that she couldn't land that final kick...until she saw Dawn walk over toShaila's unconscious figure and deliver it for her.

Chapter 12

Forty-four ounces and an extra seventeen grams is what Juice had when he finished cooking up the kilogram in Chandra's kitchen.

He bagged and pocketed the extras and gave the ounces to Kev, and they left in separate vehicles. Kev was headed to Juice's drugs houses to deliver the product to his dealers. Juice would wait for Kev at Gingko Park on 15th and Trumbull Avenue.

As Juice drove past the spot where Lil Dave and Head were murdered early this morning, he looked at the teddy bears and candles that were placed where the bodies had been. He stoppedhis Cadillac at the corner and said a silent prayer before continuing on his way.

He drove to 15th Street and Trumbull Avenue and pulled over in front of Gingko Park. There was just one woman — Veronica, a dark hued beauty Juice had known since she was justa little girl — sitting on the stone barrier next to the water fountain that everyone usually sat on. She was drinking a cold bottle of water and eating a bag of Cool Ranch Doritos. She smiled and stood to hug him when he got out of the Cadillac and walked to her with a large plastic bag in hand.

"What's up, fat guy. Where the hell you been?" she said, beaming.

"We barbecued today. Ate good, too." Juice sat down on the barrier and rubbed his belly before digging out a pack of Newports from his pocket and lighting one. "Reese came through and ate, too. Nephew wanna help me out so bad. I just can't take it. I don't like niggas lookin' at me like I owe em. I work for all my bread. I grind for this shit. Ain't givin' no handouts and I don't want none."

"Yeah, yeah, all that's fine and dandy but I couldn't get a plate?" Veronica said. "Shit, call Kela. We got a lot of leftovers. I'm sure she'll look out."

"Myyyy nigga." She raised her hand for a high-five. Juice gave it to her. They were cool likethat, more like family than friends.

Juice took a fifth of Hennessey and some clear plastic cups out of the bag. He poured a cup for Veronica and a cup for himself, and the two of them delved into conversation. She wanted to know what happened to Lil Dave and Head; Juice said he didn't know, but he'd heard that it involved the Breeds off 13th. Veronica wanted to know what had led to Jock being killed on Sawyer; Juice told her he wasn't sure, but knowing Jock's crazy ass it was probably retaliation forLil Dave and Head being murdered. Veronica was asking him had he seen Kev when Kev pulled up in his SUV a block down from them.

Kev turned into the alleyway and parked.

A twelve-year-old boy appeared from beside a garage, where four more teenage boys were standing. He jogged up to Kevin's window and then returned to his clique with a brown paper bag.

Then Kevin drove to the park and joined Veronica and Juice on the two-foot barrier. Juice poured a third cup of cognac for Kevin, and Veronica rolled a blunt of Kush in a Backwoods wrap.

As they began smoking and drinking, Juice couldn't stop himself from constantly looking in every direction. He kept thinking of Dave and Head, and how they'd had no idea that their lives were about to end until it was too late. The last thing Juice wanted to do was die on the verysame block that had made him the man he was today.

He had the Glock on his hip. It was under his loose-fitting T-shirt. He'd wanted to put the gun under his seat, just in case the police pulled up on the usual, but with the way things were going around here lately he couldn't risk not having the gun in arm's reach.

They were watching the youngsters sell the freshly cooked crack rocks when Juice received a call from his wife. Before he could answer the call, Kevin's phone rang with a call from Tara.

Both calls were about a fight the girls had had with some girl named Shaila. Juice listened intently and was proud to hear that Shawnna had come out victorious.

"Y'all stay in the damn house," Juice said when Shakela was finished talking. "Go and get that gun out of our closet in case they come back. I'll be over there in a few minutes."

"Lee, you do not have to be worried about us. I got us. We're good over here. You just bring your ass home."

"I'm out here on this money, baby."

"You need to take Reese up on whatever offer he has for you.

Quit trying to do everything yourself. Ain't nothing wrong with getting help. You'll still be a man when it's all said and done. If his help can get us in our dream home sooner, and get the girls their hair salon sooner, then damnit that's what needs to be done. Talk to that boy, Juice. Put your pride to the side and accept everything God gives you because you better believe he'll snatch that blessing right away if you don't take advantage of it."

"I'll think about it," Cup said. He coughed a couple of times, choking on the Kush smoke. A line of cars was easing through the alley where the young Vice Lords were dealing Juice's drugs. He kept looking toward them.

"You better do more than think," Shakela said. "Hurry up and get home. You know it ain't safe in those streets. It ain't even safe at a red light."

"I'm good, baby. Give me a half hour. Love you." "Love you, too, oh prideful one."

Juice couldn't repress the grin that formed as he ended the call. He shook his head andchuckled.

Then there was a loud gunshot that shocked everyone on the street into alertness. A secondlater there were eight more gunshots. It sounded close, like maybe a block or so away.

Juice looked around, reaching for his piece.

Kevin stood up, lifted his shirt, and tugged the Mac 11 out of his jeans.

Veronica's bag of Doritos (just about empty now) dropped to the ground as she leapt to herfeet and let out a frightened yelp of surprise.

A blue minivan came speeding around the corner of Drake Avenue two blocks away downfrom Gingko Park.

It was the same van that was used in Lil Dave and Head's murder, and it was coming towardTrumbull.

"Nephew," Juice said, almost involuntarily, as he snatched the gun off his hip and took aimat the minivan.

He pulled the trigger in rapid succession.

Boom, Boom, Boom, Boom, Boom...Boom, Boom, Boom.

Holes appeared in the minivan's windshield. It veered off into the Alley between Trumbull and St. Louis Avenue just as Kev opened fire, and Juice spent five more shells, stopping only because the minivan was no longer in sight.

Its driver must have lost control; there was a loud crash, then another, then a third.

Juice and Kevin ran to the alley and saw that the minivan had hit a parked car, a pickup truck, and finally a large green dumpster where it came to a stop.

In the mind to pursue the minivan, to make sure that the heartless killers inside of it were no longer a threat, Juice started forward. But then the sounds of distant screams made him turn and look toward Drake, where the minivan had come from.

Kev sent another spray of rounds at the minivan as its passenger door swung open.

A young guy with Dreadlocks was crawling out of the wrecked vehicle, his yellow T-shirt soaked in blood, an assault rifle loosely cradled in one hand.

Kev sent a third barrage of ammunition, this time not letting up until the entire 50-shot clip was depleted, and every round seemed to hit its target. The bloody-shirted man slumped back against the minivan's sliding door, rocking left and right as round after round pierced his fleshand bones.

Juice grabbed the collar of Kev's shirt and gave it a demanding yank. "Let's go, nephew," he said in an authoritative tone.

Juice ran to his car. Veronica was at his passenger door, waiting for him to unlock it with themost frightened look on her face. He hit the unlock button on his key and she got in faster thanhe did.

He sped off ahead of Kev's white Tahoe.

"Oh, my God," Veronica murmured. "Juice. What the fuck, bruh. This beef shit has gone toofar. Way too far."

Juice wasn't paying attention to Veronica. He made a right on Homan and quickly propelled the sparkling red chariot up to 16th Street, where he made another right...just as two CPD patrol cars were turning onto Trumbull.

"Brianna said it was a blue minivan," Veronica said. She gasped as the connection between the two shootings came together in her mind. "That was them...or him. I don't know. Had to be one of the boys who killed Dave and Head. I thought they had got his ass last night, that nigga Big Jay."

"They need to get out here and get some money." Juice was frustrated with all the drama. Hehad two kilos to sell, and now he would have to close down shop at his best drug spot.

It was a good thing he had four other locations that he sold his product out of. All were currently open for business, with black teenage boys dealing Juice's dope and collecting his cash for Kev to pick up.

There was a traffic jam on 16th and Drake; four cars had stopped in the middle of the street, and their drivers were gawking at a young black man's body that was stretched out in the vacant lot on the corner.

He heard one of the drivers — a chunky dark skinned woman he knew from the area — say, "That's a damn shame. Somebody done shot Zack. He wasn't even from over here. That's Tia's boyfriend. He's from up north somewhere. This shit don't make no sense."

Juice shook his head, took in a deep breath, and drove around the traffic jam.He was home minutes later.

Chapter 13

Ten Days Later

July, 14th, 2016

The shootings slowed to a crawl in the following days, mostly due to a heavy police presence in the affected areas. There were only two more shootings in North Lawndale from the fourth of July to the fourteenth, neither of which was fatal.

Juice hardly left the house. It took Kev just five days to move the first kilo and four to get rid of the second one. After putting Hector's $25,000 to the side he had $71,800 leftover for himself.

Kev and Juice's dealers had used some of their cash to buy more guns from some Indiana guy they knew. One of the guns was an AR-15 with a 120-shot drum and green laser sighting. Kev said he'd paid $1,000 for it. Juice couldn't let the opportunity to get such a weapon slide by without trying his best to get it. He ended up paying Kev $1,500 for it, and now the assault rifle was resting against the side of the living room sofa.

Furthermore, Juice had sat and talked with Reese, who wanted to do anything he could to help out the organization that had previously been run by his father. Juice's gang consisted mostly of Cup's old dealers and shooters. When Cup was in charge, the gang had been safe, for the most part. Cup had given them all the guns they needed to survive the constant wars they endured in the Windy City's cold streets; after learning of his childhood friend Dave's murder, Reese wanted to make sure that no more of his people were killed.

Which is why he'd told Juice to give him a call before he went back to the "store". That meant he wanted to add some cash of his own to Juice's next cocaine purchase. He'd also given Juice ten packets of hundred-dollar bills that amounted to $100,000. "That's for your family. Love y'all like my pops did," Reese said as he'd handed over the cash.

Juice suspected Reese's kindness had something to do with the fact that he and the twins were close all of a sudden. There had been four consecutive nights when the twins had gone out with Reese. He'd gotten Shawnna a new vehicle, a black 2017 Dodge Challenger on 26-inchDUB rims, and he'd bought Dawn the 26-inch Forgiato rims she now had on her Charger.

As much as Juice hated what was happening, he felt that as the father of two eighteen-year- old queens, he had to fall back and let the girls make their own decisions. He and Shakela had raised them well. They knew how to conduct themselves like ladies. He worried a little about Shawnna, the wild card that she was, but he knew the girls were wise beyond their years.

The only thing bothering Juice was that Chandra had started hanging out with the twins. He didn't like that at all.

It was a quarter past noon, the warmest day of the month so far. Juice had just returned home from a morning-long search of possible building rentals for his daughters' hair salon. Shakelawas with him, running her mouth about the exorbitant prices of the salon locations as theyentered their bedroom and prepared for some quality time in bed.

"I just don't understand how they expect somebody to spend so much on a fucking lease.

Jesus Christ." Shakela kicked off her Chanel heels and climbed in bed.

"It'll be worth it." Juice sat down next to her and put his smartphone on the charger. "Our bank will finance the loan. I'll put the $20,000 cash down. It'll be fine. Stop stressing over it. I hustle just for situations like this. Trust me, our babies are going to be A-okay."

Shakela crossed her arms over the chest of her Bulls crop top and studied Juice through squinted eyelids. Her denim booty shorts were as tight and short as can be.

To Juice, she looked good enough to eat.

He turned and stretched out next to her. A groan of relaxation escaped him. "I'm not getting out of this bed for at least four hours," he said as he took off his Jordan sneakers and dropped them on the floor.

"You got twenty grand to put down on that salon by yourself?" Shakela asked. "Because us moving into the new place comes first."

"No, it doesn't. The kids come first."

"Yeah, okay. They need a house to live in before they can get a business.""They got a house right here."

"They share a bedroom, Juice. Let's be serious here. They are grown as fuck now. What if one of them gets pregnant? They need their own space."

"If one of them gets pregnant..." Juice didn't know how to conclude the threat. He shook his head. "None of that matters anyway. I have the down payment for the house, too. We're putting up ten and ten, right? Twenty thousand?"

"Yes. We talked about this." She paused; then, "Really, you should just put it all up and let me keep my lil ten bands. You got way more money saved up than I do."

Shakela folded her legs Indian-style and picked up her iPad. She went to a saved bookmark in her browser that took her straight to the quarter-million-dollar home they were hoping to purchase on Zillow.com.

"I'm not doing it all by myself," Juice said. He wasn't about to pay for the salon and the new home all by himself. "Marriage is fifty-fifty," he argued. "You pay your half, I pay mine."

"Are you forgetting that I was there in the kitchen when Reese gave you that money? That's an extra hundred grand, on top of all the thousands of dollars Kev keeps bringing you. I'm not dumb, Lee. Stop being cheap and get the things we need to grow as a family and as a couple."

"They can ask Reese for the salon...since he wanna buy cars and rims and shit." Juice sat up in bed and looked at the screen of Kela's iPad.

"You sound foolish, Juice. You ought to be glad he bought Shawnna that car." "I am happy," Juice said, sounding the exact opposite of happy.

Shakela flipped through the photos of the house they had been looking at for the past few weeks. It was a five-bedroom two-story home not far from where they lived now. The best part about it was that the house was in a relatively peaceful area where gang violence was not an issue. Juice planned to move the family there. They would rent out this house, which he'd fully purchased two years prior for $80,000 cash. He paid the eighty grand with drug money he'dmade that summer.

"We need to have a talk." Shakela shut off the iPad. Her eyes rolled up, and her head made aslow turn to him; he knew then that he was in trouble.

"Aww shit," Juice muttered under his breath. He'd sensed the tension since around noon.

"You're damn right 'aww shit'. What the fuck is up with you and that bitch Chandra? You fuckin' my best friend's daughter?" Shakela crossed her arms tightly. Her jaw muscles flexed as she gritted her teeth and scowled at him.

"What?" Juice put on a look of surprise. "What are you talking about?"

"You know damn well what I'm talking about. A friend of mine inboxed me on Facebook saying she heard you and Chandra been fuckin' around."

Juice waved off the gossip. "I don't wanna hear nothin' about what somebody else heard. That's some bullshit. Do you honestly think that — if I did cheat on you — I would do it with your best friend's daughter? Come on now, baby. You know I'm smarter than that."

"What's that supposed to mean?" Shakela was replete with attitude.

"It just means I'm not cheating on you, not with your friend's daughter, not with anybody.

Okay? Are we clear on this?"

Shakela sucked her teeth and lifted her eyes up in their sockets again. Juice laughed and kissed her on the cheek. She didn't throw a punch like she usually did when she had solid proof that he'd done something wrong. That was a good thing.

"I love you, baby. Don't listen to no gossip over me." His grin widened as he became more relieved. He pecked his lips on her temple and wrapped an arm around her shoulders, pulling her close.

"Whatever, Lee,' she said, sniffling as she began to cry. She didn't pull away from Juice. Instead, she shifted onto her side and lay her head on his chest. "Don't fucking cheat on me. Please. That's all I ask. If I find out it's true, Lee. If I find out it's true...ugh, I can't stand you sometimes. I hope you wore a condom if you did fuck that nasty lil girl."

"I ain't fucked nobody but you.""Mmm hmm."

Juice felt his heart pounding. He'd almost been caught.Just then, his smartphone rang.

It was Hector calling. He knew it not because of a recognized number but because of its 956 area code. Hector changed phones on an almost weekly basis, and he always used the area code of his hometown, Brownsville, Texas.

Juice was grateful for the interruption. He picked up the phone and answered.

"Got some good news," Hector said. "Can you meet me at the silver bean in an hour?""Yup, on my way," Juice said.

He hurried out of bed and stepped into his sneakers.

"This shit ain't over, Lee," Shakela shouted after Juice as he rushed out of the bedroom.

Chapter 14

"Take your glasses off. Get comfortable. Make yourself at home," Marlo said, staring at Shaila's backside as he shut and locked his apartment door.

Shaila got comfortable, but she wasn't going to remove her shades. The dark lenses hid her bruised eyes. Her face was still healing from the beat-down Shawnna gave her on the fourth, but Marlo didn't seem to care. She'd met him on Facebook about six months ago. This was their first face-to-face encounter, and he did not disappoint. Marlo was just as handsome and clean as he appeared on social media. She was supposed to be here to buy an ounce of OG Kush from him. The money was in her pocket, but Shaila didn't think she'd need it. Marlo was thirsty; he was staring way too hard at her short little black miniskirt. He had rubbed on her butt twice since he picked her up from. It was evident that in his mind he was getting the pussy.

Marlo was not what you would call a baller but he definitely had a little money. Looking around the apartment, there were several things that caught Shaila's eye. The shiny hardwood floors, the massive widescreen Smart TV on the wall, the hundreds of Xbox One games packed into a glass-doored cabinet next to the TV. The apartment was in the West Englewood neighborhood, on 63rd and Paulina.

Shaila followed a number of men she considered to be well-off on social media, and Marlo was one of them. He was one of those attention-seeking souls who posted photos of the ounces and pounds of high-grade marijuana he sold to his Instagram page. He had a gray E350 Mercedes Benz. He had what appeared to be a Rolex watch on one wrist, and a thick gold chain hanging down from his slender neck. He was as skinny as they came and about six feet tall, wearing an expensive designer outfit and shoulder-length dreadlocks.

This come up would be a piece of cake. Free money.

"I got into a fight a few weeks ago," Shaila said, taking a seat on his sofa. "My eyes are still a little bruised and sore. It's better if I keep my sunglasses on."

She didn't mention that she'd also lost two premolar teeth in the fight, and that her mouthstill ached miserably.

Shaila didn't have a dollar to her name but she didn't look like it. The other day she and an old classmate of hers had boosted a bunch of clothes from the Woodfield Mall. Shaila was wearing one of the new outfits, and it fit her perfectly. She'd put on some of her sister's makeup and a pair of her sister's new-looking high heels. Truth be told, Shaila was flat broke; the money she'd brought to pay for the weed was cash she'd taken out of her sister's purse. But Shaila knew that as long as there were men who couldn't turn down a girl with a peach-shaped ass she had a way to get back on her feet.

The only thing that wasn't up to par was her hair. She'd greased and combed it and threw itin a tight ponytail, and she hoped it was good enough to keep Marlo's eyes on her.

It was working so far.

Marlo went to the kitchen and returned with two glasses of ice and a bottle of Remy Martin. As he sat down next to Shaila and poured up, he kept sneaking glances at her thighs and biting down on his lower lip.

Shaila played the innocent role, smiling coyly and keeping her eyes on her smartphone. She sent out a couple of text messages and scrolled through her Facebook news feed.

"You got some sexy ass lips," Marlo said. "I remember when you first started following me on IG. I saw how fat that ass was and instantly followed you back."

"It's still fat, nigga."

"Not like it was back then."

"Yeah, but it's getting there. I'll be back to my old weight by the end of summer."

"Fuck with me and you'll be back to it even sooner than that. I'm eating good. My whole team is. You need to be fucking with me."

"I wouldn't be here if I wasn't." Shaila crossed her legs and set the smartphone down on her lap. She drank half of her cup of Remy in two big gulps.

Marlo left the room again. This time he returned with a digital scale and three large plastic bags full of marijuana. The bags contained at least a pound in each. He was showing off. There was no need to bring out so much weed when all Shaila wanted to buy was an ounce.

"See," he said, beaming. "I told you I do this shit. I got loud for days in this bitch, straight from Cali. You wanna smoke first?"

Shaila shrugged her shoulders and set her purse aside. The purse was a Chanel, stolen duringa downtown smash-and-grab Darren and his guys pulled off this past January.

"I don't know how you're able to keep so much weed here in this apartment. Niggas are sotreacherous nowadays, especially out here. I'd be scared to keep anything here if I were you."

"Scared? Scared of who? These niggas ain't on shit. They know better than to fuck with me.

Last nigga tried to rob me got changed in broad daylight. I'm with the shits for real."

"I'm just saying." Another shrug from Shaila. Marlo gave her a blunt wrap and put a few buds of the loud on the table in front of her. She rolled the blunt while he weighed up the ounce.

"Do you know how long I've wanted to fuck you?" Marlo said. "I wanna see what thatmouth do, too. I know it's serious."

"You don't know shit." Shaila laughed. She lit the blunt, took a couple of hits, and then swallowed another mouthful of the Remy as she passed the blunt to him.

"I got a mixtape about to drop in a few days," Marlo said. "Juggin and Drillin Volume Two. Shit's hard as fuck, on David. I got a couple features on that bitch. Katie Got Bands on there. I tried to get Dreezy to fuck with me but I guess she was too busy working with Gucci Mane."

"Dreezy is the hardest female rapper in the game right now. That new album is the shit. I heard, like, three tracks off it. She went hard."

"If you think that's hard you gon' love my mixtape. Make sure you share it on your page when it drops."

Shaila nodded her head. "I gotchoo."

Marlo kept talking about his mixtape and the 'real' Rolex watch he had on until the blunt wasjust a tiny little roach. Then he turned his attention to Shaila and slipped a hand under her miniskirt.

She wasn't wearing underwear; he sank a finger in her pussy

and did a ‘come here’ motion.

Shaila was already wet and ready to fuck.

“Let’s go in the bedroom,” she said, standing up. “I’ll show you what these sexy ass lips can

do.”

Marlo was all smiles as he got up and led Shaila to his bed-room. She stepped over a white

pit bull puppy that was running around the kitchen.

“Look,” Marlo said with a laugh, “he wanna fuck, too.” He lifted the back of her miniskirtand squeezed her ass.

Shaila shook her head. She hoped Marlo wasn’t going to pull out a four-inch dick and act like he was the shit with it.

So much for being hopeful.

He unbuckled his Hermes belt and pulled out his magic stick, only his stick wasn’t so magical. It was a curved couple of inches, already rock-hard.

Shaila almost rolled her eyes as she got down on her knees. She took his entire little lengthin her mouth and started sucking.

“Aw, hell yeah,” he said. “Deepthroat this big muhfucka then. Mmm.” It took every ounce of restraint in Shaila not to laugh out loud.

She had him sit on the bed. He took a gun off his waist and put it behind him on the bed. Wanting to impress and relax him, she serviced him the way she used to do the tricks who spent good money with her, before her coke habit habit had caused her to fall off. She spit on his phallus and sealed her lips snugly around it as she hurriedly moved her head forward and back.

“I’ma bless you nicely for this,” he said.

“Hold on one minute.” Shaila stood up, still stroking him. “Let me pee right quick. Where’s the bathroom.”

“Go through the kitchen. Straight to the back. And hurry up.”

“Okay. Be right back.” Shaila spoke quickly and exited the room even quicker.

She went to the back door and unlocked it, then calmly walked into the bathroom and shut the door. She’d already sent Darren the address. Now all she needed to do was tell him the back door was unlocked. Then she could jump back in bed with Marlo and wait.

Darren would take care of the rest.

When Shaila returned to the bedroom Marlo had turned on some slow music. He had movedhis gun; it now lay atop his boxers and pants on the floor beside the bed.

He was jerking his mini penis.

"Put this muhfucka back in ya throat for a minute," he said, grinning widely.This time Shaila didn't hold in the laugh.

Chapter 15

The AK-47 assault rifle Darren had in hand was the same weapon that had taken the lives ofHead and Lil Dave.

He tiptoed into the kitchen, leaving the back door open. He wore a black ski mask and a thingray hoody, and there was duct tape on the heels of his Air Force Ones.

The text he'd gotten from Shaila read: 'Back door open, we'll be in bedroom. Be careful. Ilove you.'

Darren took a calming breath.

Then he went in search of the bedroom.

He found it seconds later and burst in with the assault rifle raised to fire.

Shaila was riding Marlo when the door came swinging open. She immediately rolled off the bed and picked up Marlo's pistol before what was going down could even register in his mind.

She aimed the gun at his face.

"Where's the stash?" Shaila asked Marlo as she pulled her mini-skirt down to cover her nakedness.

"Run that shit, nigga," Darren said through clenched teeth.

Marlo was instantly frightened. He raised his trembling hands over his head in surrender. "Y'all ain't gotta shoot me. You can have that shit. Just let me live, fam." Marlo's voice was

cracking. It was obvious that he feared an imminent death. "It's all in the shoe boxes in mycloset. Sixty-five thousand, and another pound o' bud in. Three pounds on the living room table. That's all I have. On my life, fam. That's everything."

"Bitch, get a bag and grab that shit," Darren said to Shaila. He kept his eyes and the long barrel of the AK-47 trained on Marlo's face.

Shaila dug in her purse and took out the trash bags she'd brought along just for this purpose. She also had a black ski mask and a pair of gloves, which she put on immediately. She first went to the living and got the three pounds, then she came back to the bedroom and ransacked the cash-filled shoe boxes in Marlo's closet.

"Just don't kill me, family," Marlo pleaded. "I won't come after you, I won't try nothin'. I swear. Just let me—"

BOOM BOOM BOOM.

A three-round burst of ammunition hit Marlo high in the forehead, leaving the back of his skull and his brains clinging to the headboard. He slumped over stiffly on his pillow.

The gunshots didn't faze Shaila. She kept right on emptying shoe boxes full of rubberbanded cash into the trash bag. Darren helped her with the last two boxes. He took the goldwatch off Marlo's wrist and pocketed it.

Shaila led the way out to the stolen car they had waiting outback. She rushed into the backseat with Darren.

Kobe, Darren's friend and fellow gang member, was behind the wheel. He took off as soon as Darren's door was closed. Shaila slithered her way between her seat and the back of the passenger seat, cradling the garbage bag and Marlo's Glock 17 pistol to her chest.

Darren kept his ski mask on. They had succeeded in robbing Marlo but they weren't in the clear just yet. They were out of bounds, Black Gangsters in a neighborhood full of Gangster Disciples, Black P Stones, and Black Disciples.

There was a trio of young black men standing on the corner. Neither of them reacted to seeing him in the mask. They could not have been gang members, but Darren kept an eye on them just in case. He didn't take off the mask until they were soaring down Ashland a moment later.

"Y'all rob him?" Kobe asked. "What was up with those gunshots?"

"We got a lil bud and a couple bands," Darren said. He grabbed Shaila's hand and pulled her up onto the backseat. "Enough to buy some more guns. I got a stack for you just for driving. I'll give you another thousand when you get back in good with Shawnna."

"Shawnna ain't fuckin' with me, G. On Black Gangsta. She on some other nigga now. I heardher and her twin sister fuckin' with Bankroll Reese. You know I ain't got a chance with her after that rich ass dude. I can't outdo him."

Darren rolled the ski mask up to his forehead. "Buy her some roses, or somethin' sweet like that. Trust me, it'll work. Girls love shit like that."

"It's true," Shaila added. That was all. She was too afraid for her life and excited about the money to say anything else. She took off her gloves and put them and the gun on her lap as she eased up onto the seat.

Kobe was driving about ten miles over the speed limit as they were approaching Ashland Avenue and Garfield Boulevard.

"G, slow down," Darren said. "Don't fuck around and get us pulled over."

"My bad, bruh." Darren slowed the stolen gray Ford Taurus just as they were passing the White Castle restaurant.

Which is when another shooting occurred.

A small red Honda pulled into the White Castle parking lot alongside a white SUV, and someone inside of the Honda riddled the SUV's driver door with bullets before racing away.

"Man, they just blew dude's ass down," Kobe murmured in disbelief. He drove slowly past what was more than likely a fresh homicide scene. "At least it'll take the heat off us."

"Wow," Shaila said, stunned by the sudden gunfire.

"Damn." Darren shook his head. "Just another day in Chiraq."

Chapter 16

"This is how our house is going to look one day. Foreign cars sitting in front of a mansion, abig-ass lawn, a swimming pool. This is the life, sis. It really is."

Dawn's wishful voice and the gentle chirping of birds were the only sounds Shawnna heard. She and Dawn had their butts resting against the chromed out grille of a white Rolls-Royce Phantom in front of Bankroll Reese's ten-million-dollar mansion. Situated on a prominent intersection in the exclusive Chicago suburb of Burr Ridge, the home had a gold Jerusalem limestone exterior done in neo-Byzantine Moorish revival. The interior, appointed in Brazilian wood and Italian marble, featured nine fireplaces, a 20-car basement garage, and a high-ceilingedballroom.

There were three other vehicles in the circular drive: a black Lamborghini Gallardo, ayellow Lamborghini Aventador, and a black Rolls-Royce Wraith. In the basement garage there were twelve more luxury vehicles

Reese was gone to take care of some business in his Bentley Bentayga. He was due back anyminute.

"I can't believe people are requesting us to host all these club events," Shawnna said. Shewas scrolling through her emails on her new Samsung Galaxy S7. Ever since she and Dawn had started hanging out with Bankroll Reese they'd become the center of attention in Chicago. Everyone wanted them in some kind of video, or to promote some product on social media, or to host some sort of gathering. Most were offering good pay, and the Wilkins twins had accepted a select few late-night club hosting gigs; the twins ignored the cheapskate offers. They weren't going to shortchange themselves. Reese had gotten them roles as lead models in Gucci Mane's latest music video, which they'd just finished yesterday in Birmingham, Alabama. After buying them dozens of matching designer outfits, purses, and heels and taking them to get their hair and nails done, Reese had taken the twins to the video shoot without telling them what they were about to do. Shawnna was geeked when they arrived at the video shoot; Dawn had been shy, but neither of them managed to disappoint the video director, a fat black man who could not stop commenting on how beautiful the two of them looked.

Then there was the trip to New York City, where Reese introduced them to Jamie Foxx, Tyrese Gibson, and a host of other Hollywood celebs during an evening dinner at someone's enormous mansion. They'd hit up Sue's Rendezvous in Mount Vernon and helped Reese throw thousands of dollars in singles at the strippers.

Thumbing through $10,000 in hundreds (another gift from Reese), Shawnna was as happy as she'd ever been. She had on a white Gucci dress — the pleated Gabardine mini — and black Giuseppe Zanotti six-inch heels. Dawn had on the same dress but her Giuseppe heels were silver and gold.

"What do you plan on doing with your ten thousand?" Dawn asked, twirling a strand of her long black hair around a finger. "I think we should go ahead and get the salon ourselves. We might as well get it in order now. Twenty thousand dollars and a bank loan for about eightygrand should get us everything we need for the salon. Daddy will take care of any extras. We can rent out some booths and get that extra cash on the side. We can do hair all day long when we want to or we don't even have to show up for work at all. Either way it goes we'll be pretty much set for life as long as we keep the business up and running. If Reese wants to be helpful and hitus with some more bands, we'll open another salon up north. We have to make every dollar workfor us, sis. We can't be content with being in some rich nigga's shadow and then going home withnothing more than a bunch of good memories and designer clothes when he's done using us. Ifwe play our cards right and work hard enough, with or without Reese's help we'll be good when it's all said and done. Are you with me on this?"

"I'm with you, sis." Shawnna said, nodding her head in agreement. "With the club hostings and doing hair all the time we'll have more than enough for at least the first salon."

"Yeah, and maybe we'll be able to get Reese and some of these other millionaire celebrities we've been meeting lately to invest in a few more of our salons."

"Great minds think alike." Shawnna high-fived Dawn, then they left the driveway and went around to the side of the mansion to an outside swimming pool that had instantly become Dawn and Shawnna's favorite place at the luxurious Villa Taj (an Italian-Persian mix meaning "crown jewel country residence"). The pool was massive. It had a 15-foot water slide, numerous fountains, and a waterfall cave that the twins loved to relax in. With 30,000 feet of luxurious living space, the Villa Taj was definitely the largest home either of the twins had ever seen.

They removed their heels and sat on the edge of the swimming pool with their feet in the water. Dawn raised her own Galaxy S7 and showed a bright smile. "Do it for Snapchat, bitch," she said, and snapped a quick selfie of the two of them. Two short videos followed.

"Have you talked to Cage since we got back from New York?" Shawnna asked.

Dawn rolled her eyes, then returned them to Instagram as the selfie she'd just taken was uploading. "Cage and I are good. I need to be asking you about that nigga Kobe. What's up with y'all? Chandra said he's been looking for you since around the first of this month. Have you told him about Reese?"

"First of all," Shawnna said, and sucked her teeth, "it ain't none of Kobe's business what I doand who I do it with. I am a very grown, very single boss bitch, okay? I does what I does when I does it and I could give two fucks who likes it. Secondly, I don't give a damn how long he's beenlooking for me. His ass shouldn't have slept with that trifling bitch on Sawyer. Had that hoe coming to our house with that shit."

"She came to our house because you shot at her, Shawnna," Dawn said matter-of-factly. "I'd have gone to a bitch's house about that, too."

"Well, you would've got whooped just like that hoe got whooped. Simple as that."Dawn sighed. "I'm just asking about Kobe. You ain't gotta get all crazy with me."

"I'm not getting crazy. What I'm doing is telling you what it is and what it's not. That boy don't run my life."

"Would you ever give him another chance?""Hell to the no."

"Yeah, right. You say that now. I know you, Shawnna. I know you better than anybody else knows you. You love Kobe too much.

If he pulled up right now I'd bet my whole ten grand you would hop your happy ass right in the car with him."

"Call him and find out." Shawnna wasn't trying to argue about her feelings for Kobe.She had her sights set on Bankroll Reese.

For almost two whole weeks now Shawnna had been with Reese just about every single day and night. She'd watched him have sex with two of the strippers they'd left Sue's Rendezvous with in New York City and a girl in Chicago she'd never before seen. All of the girls looked like models, with big round asses like Shawnna and Dawn's and bottomless sexual appetites. Jealousy raged through Shawnna's veins just thinking about it. She could have easily been the one Reese was fucking. The only thing holding her back was Dawn, who insisted that fucking Reese would make him change the way he treated them.

"He already has all kinds of gold-diggers chasing after him on a daily basis," Dawn had said. "Give him the pussy on your own terms. Make him wait it out. Make him appreciate the person you are before you let him sample your goods. That's what a real woman would do."

Shawnna wasn't really onboard with Dawn's idea but she had no choice; the one time sheand Reese had gotten some alone time together in the mansion's theater the other night, Reesehad turned her down, stating that he was too drunk. He'd left the theater for one of the mansion's eleven bathrooms. Shawnna had walked past the closed bathroom door and heard him vomiting and heaving. The twins had been with Reese for five out of the last ten days. There hadn't been a lot of situations where Shawnna and Reese were alone together. Next time, she promised herself,it was going to go down.

She swung her feet back and forth in the cool blue water, while Dawn sifted through the hundreds upon hundreds of direct messages that had been sent to their Instagram page. Both of them were surprised by the number of famous names that were checking for them. There were two Chicago Bulls players, along with twelve more messages from the verified Instagram accounts of other NBA players. A famous music producer in Atlanta wanted to take them out on a date. A popular Chicago rap artist, an Atlanta rap group, and the R&B star who'd been the twins' biggest crush for years — all of them wanted to meet and hang out with Shawnna and Dawn now.

"I never could've imagined that so many celebrities would be after us like this," Dawn said, smiling from ear to ear. Just as she always did when she got nervous, she began rubbing her right thigh. "I might have to sit Cage down for a talk about this. We might need to start seeing other people."

Shawnna laughed once. "Yeah, okay. Like I'm gonna believe that. You love Cage's dirty drawers."

"If he had dirty drawers we wouldn't be together now, so you can kill that," Dawn fired back. "I think he's still fucking his ex, anyway. Might as well do me for a while."

"Don't lie to yourself, sis. You wouldn't cheat on Cage to save your life. Not even if it was Bulletface, your favorite rapper."

"Yeah, but I want to. That has to count for something."

Shawnna rolled her eyes and lifted herself to her feet. "Let's get drunk, bitch. We're at this big ass mansion just sitting here. Let's have some fun. I got about a quarter ounce of that good weed left in my purse, too. We're supposed to be on the moon by now."

"I'm with you when you're right," Dawn said as Shawnna helped her up. "Let's get rock star wasted."

"Can I join in?" Reese asked.

Shawnna and Dawn gasped in unison. Neither of them had heard Bankroll Reese walk up. He was standing right behind them with a thick cigar in his mouth, a bottle of Patrón tequila in his left hand, and three pint-sized bottles of purple Actavis syrup in his other hand. He wore a black and gold Versace robe, and a bunch of gold and diamond jewelry. Chubb and Suwu and a third guy the twins knew from North Lawndale as Lil Luke were walking up behind Reese, carrying sleeves of Styrofoam cups, big gold bottles of Ace of Spades champagne, and large plastic bottles of Fanta and Sprite sodas.

Looking past him, Shawnna saw that there was a party bus behind his Bentley SUV.

A long line of women was exiting the bus wearing bikinis and swimsuits. They had towels and beach balls. A few of them even had water guns, the large Super Soaker kind. There were some familiar faces among the group of women, namely Myesha, the twins' best friend, Chandra, Tamera and Tirzah, and Kevin's wife Tara. They were all headed for the pool.

"The city was dry," Reese said, slipping his arms around Shawnna and Dawn's waists, "so I brought the party to us."

Chapter 17

The first text message was an explicitly worded threat:

'I swear on my mother's grave Lee if I find out you fucked that girl its on and popping and you know I'm not fucking playing I'll kill you and that bitch you got me so fucked up for real I'll beat her ass like Shawnna beat up that girl the other week now try me and see if I'm fucking playing.'

Seven additional text messages came after the first one, but Juice ignored them. He had a meeting with the man who made sure he had food on his table and a roof over his head. The argument with Shakela would have to wait.

He set the phone down on the circular black table and put on his sunglasses. He was sitting at one of the many tables the AT&T Plaza at Millennium Park offered to Chicagoans and visiting tourists who wanted to enjoy a nice view of the magnificently sculpted "silver bean" while eating lunch and socializing.

Juice had a huge meal, a KFC bucket full of chicken and all the available sides. His lips and fingertips were greasy when Hector walked up and took a seat across from him, so instead of the usual handshake they nodded their greetings.

"What is this, our third meeting here?" Hector said, smiling as he looked around at the hundred or so other park visitors. "It's a great place to be on a beautiful day like this. I tell you what, if my wife wasn't nagging me half to death about some girl down the street from us hitting on me I might have brought her along with me."

"I'm going through some bullshit with my wife, too."

"About what? That pretty little thing you had in the car with you last time I saw you?"

Juice nodded his head. "Some chick on Facebook told her. She ain't got no proof, though.

Just speculation. Bullshit speculation. But still, I might have to cut Chandra off."

The gold cross on Hector's thin gold necklace glittered in the sunlight. He had on a white button-up shirt and slacks. Juice thought he looked a lot like the guy who played Pablo Escobar on Narcos, his favorite show on Netflix.

"You know," Hector said, reaching into the bucket of chicken for a drumstick, "I've never cheated on my old lady. You black guys are always so quick to cheat on your women. It's notlike that with Mexicans. We cherish our señoritas. They're worth more than gold to us, because with all the crap we go through we can always count on them to be there for the family. Don't getme wrong, people cheat everywhere, just not like you guys do. Not to be labeled as a player. But hey, to each its own. Just don't let it affect our business."

"It won't." Juice moved back in his seat, picking up his large KFC cup of iced Pepsi. He put the straw between his lips and drank, studying Hector, wondering what the trip to Mexico was all about. Probably some cartel business, like a scene right out of Narcos.

'I watch too much Narcos', Juice thought to himself. "Had any luck with that second one?" Hector asked.

"It's gone. Been waiting on you. And I brought that twenty-five I owe you."

"Well, I've got good news. Great news, actually. Probably the best news you've heard all year. You're gonna love me for this."

Hector paused for effect and rubbed his belly. A pigeon landed on the edge of the dark green shade umbrella that sprouted from the center of their table, flicked its head around sporadically, and then took flight. Hector moved forward until he was leaning over the table.

"I unexpectedly ran into four times the amount of product I usually get. My guy...the guy I deal with in Mexico...he's very rich. Very, very rich. So insanely rich that he has a home worth over a hundred million dollars!" Hector spoke in an excited whisper. His eyes were wide. He gripped the sides of the table with his thick brown hands. Darren had never seen Hector look so serious. "To make a long story short, he offered me more product, and lowered the price I have to pay for each one of those shirts. I've got two hundred and fifty of them on the market."

Shirts were of course kilos of cocaine. Juice was waiting for the good news.

"From now on you can get them for just twenty-five bucks each." $25,000 each. "Now, what I'd advise you to do is focus on expanding your reach throughout this region. Find some guys in Indiana, in Ohio, in Michigan. All those guys we did time with back in the day. Lock down the midwest first. There's a ton of untapped cash here. Head down south if you need to, or hit upNew York. I saw your daughters in New York on Jamie Foxx's Snapchat just the other night.My, how they've grown since you had those pictures of them in the joint. I bet they get all the attention."

"What the hell you doing on Snapchat?"

Grinning, Hector took a smartphone off his hip and turned on its screen. "Gotta get with thetimes, my friend. All the youngsters are on it. My kids are on it. Yours are probably on it, too."

"I don't give a damn about no Snapchat. Not unless it can cut me a Snapcheck. I'm tryna getrich, nigga."

Hector found this to be incredibly funny. He laughed and laughed until he choked on a piece of chicken he hadn't finished chewing. Juice got up and patted him on the back.

"You good, Hector?"

Hector nodded, tears falling down his corpulent face as he tried to get the laughter under control.

"Don't die on me before you give me them shirts," Juice said as he returned to his seat. "I know you can give em to me for less than that twenty-five, too. Stop being so tight. Let a real nigga get rich with you."

"Okay." Hector wiped his face. "Okay, how does this sound? When you're able to get up enough cash to bring me...let's say a hundred and ninety bucks. You bring me that and I'll give you ten shirts. That's cutting into my profits but I need it right now. The wife wants a new Mercedes, and so does my son."

"Deal. I'll bring it to you tonight."

Hector cocked his head to the side and knitted his brows. "You mean to tell me you've got the whole hundred and ninety right now?"

"No. Only missing about ten bucks, though. I know somebody who'll loan it to me. I'm goodfor it."

"You've got yourself a deal." Hector reached across the table and shook Juice's hand, sealingthe lucrative drug deal.

Ten kilos of cocaine for $190,000.

Now Juice was ready to start wholesaling the coke, and he would charge no less than

$38,000 per kilo. He knew at least one person to whom he could more than likely sell every kilogram. If not then he had hundreds of men from the west side streets to choose from, men whoneeded kilos to supply cocaine and crack in every neighborhood and apartment complex they controlled. He knew gang leaders from all over the city, men he'd gone to school with and their children who also sold every drug they could get their hands on. Either way it went the ten kilos would not last long. He'd be right back to Hector for another ten kilos. Once he made it to a million dollars in cash he would retire from drug-dealing and go legit.

Juice was officially in the big league. As long as he steered clear of the the dangerous areas in the hood and stuck to supplying the streets with Hector's coke, he knew for certain that the lifestyle he'd always wanted was within reach.

He'd be a millionaire in no time.

Hector dug in his pants pocket and took out a folded piece of yellow paper. "Here's the cash drop address. Meet me there with it in two hours. I'll have your shirts. Try not to have one ofyour girlfriends in the car with you this time, eh? And don't drive the Cadi with the rims." Hectorslid the paper across the table. "Back of my aunt's restaurant in Little Village. Taqueria Los Comales, on 26th and Troy. Just pull into the parking lot. I'll have a couple of guys with me, just in case, you know. This is a lot of cash we're dealing with. Wouldn't want any discrepancies."

Juice picked up the address and dropped it in his KFC bag.

"Catch you later, ése. Bring that twenty-five with you when you come with the dough." Hector took another drumstick of the delicious chicken out of the KFC bucket before turning andstrolling away with half of his attention on a Snapchat video.

Juice laughed at the funny old Mexican. Hector had to be at least fifty years old, maybe a few years younger or older, Juice couldn't be sure because Hector never revealed much about himself aside from the fact that he'd been born in Mexico and raised somewhere in Texas. Juice had learned in prison that Hector was affiliated with Sur 13 and the Mexican Mafia but that was all he knew, and he wasn't trying to learn more. The only thing Juice wanted to know was how he could get more 1008-gram bricks of coke to supply the streets with.

He got up, trashed his leftovers, and left when Hector was out of sight. When Juice got in hisCadillac he looked around its interior and muttered, "Fuckin' Mexican. Hatin' on my Cadillac. Y'all probably came to this country in a Honda Accord — ninety-nine of you lil short, funny- talkin' muhfuckas — but you wanna hate on the Cadi."

Juice was shaking his head and dialing Bankroll Reese's number as he accelerated up Michigan Avenue in the candy red Cadillac on big chrome rims.

The first person Juice would try selling the bricks of coke to was Reese, and he hoped the flashy young millionaire would buy all of them.

Chapter 18

Kobe knocked on Shaila's bedroom door for the fourth time since they'd arrived at the apartment building twenty minutes earlier. "Why y'all hiding the loot? Let me in on that shit."

"Hold on, nigga! Damn!" Shaila shouted.

She was on her bed, stuffing her and Darren's cash back into the trash bag while Darrenstood at her dresser and weighed up four ounces of OG Kush for Kobe. The $10,000 in cash Kobe was getting for his role in the robbery was stacked up next to the digital scale in two neat piles of hundreds and fifties. It had been easy to add up the cash; the bundles of bills were all rubber-banded together with pieces of paper behind the bands that told him how much was in each bundle. Kobe's take from the robbery was a hundred fifty-dollar bills, fifty hundred-dollar bills, and a quarter pound of Kush.

"Here I come, G," Darren said, loud enough for Kobe to hear him through the door. "I'm gettin' this shit together now."

A long-legged kick from lanky 18-year-old Jacoby splintered the doorframe and sent Shaila's door flying open.

Instinctively, Shaila picked up the Glock she'd taken from Marlo and aimed it at Kobe. Darren waved for her to lower the gun as he moved from the dresser and got between her and Kobe.

"Shoot me, bitch." Kobe's expression became fierce. "You ain't gon' shoot shit. Better put that gun down before I get on what I'm always on."

Reluctantly — almost too reluctantly — Shaila moved the gun off to her left side; she didn't put it down.

"You kicked my fucking door open, asshole! Hope you know that's coming out of your money," Shaila said, reaching for the stack of hundreds Darren had put to the side for Kobe.

Darren grabbed the money before Shaila could. He turned and handed the cash and a Ziploc bag of Kush that weighed exactly 114 Grams on the scale.

"Gave you two extra grams for the bag weight," Darren said as Kobe started counting the stack of hundreds. "That's a Q.P. and ten bands. Five in hundreds and five in fifties. We did allthe work so we got more. I'll pay for the door. Chill out, bruh. Shit ain't that serious."

"Get him out of my apartment, D. Please. I'd really fucking appreciate it," Shaila mutteredwith little conviction.

Darren could tell that Kobe wanted to do something to Shaila. He saw it in Kobe's scowl.

"We ain't about to be fighting each other," Darren said, looking from Kobe to Shaila and back to Kobe. "Only enemies we got is them niggas on 15th. We need to be buying up every gunwe can find, and Kobe, you need to be getting that bitch Shawnna on the phone. That's the only reason I put you in on this lick in the first place. You gotta get back in good with her. Especially since she done got with the millionaire nigga. It's gotta be some money in that house on Central Park. Her daddy got that bread, and I'll bet everything I got that he had somethin' to do with bro n'em gettin' whacked. They killed B Man on the fourth. What's today, the fourteenth? They whacked one of the realest Breeds in the game ten days ago. Somebody gotta die for that, G. Andwe gotta cut the head off. The head is Juice, your girlfriend's daddy. Let's get our straps up and rob him. We can whack him and take everything. If you come in with me I'll split it even with you, but not if all you're gon' do is be a getaway driver. Put in that work like me and Shaila just did."

"Nigga, you know all the work I put in for this mob," Kobe said, turning to leave. "I'll get Shawnna back. And I'll try to make sure she don't pumpkin-head your girl again."

Kobe chuckled once as he left out the door he'd just kicked in.

Gritting her teeth tightly together, Shaila raised the gun again and aimed it at the spot where Kobe had stood seconds prior.

All Darren could do was laugh. He walked Kobe to the front door, told Kobe to just leave and call him later, and shut the door when Kobe was down the stairs and out the door. When he returned to the bedroom Shaila dumped the trash bag in the center of her bed. The cash they weresplitting and three big bags of Kush. The fourth bag of Kush was open on the dresser.

"I'm about to go take a shower," Shaila said. "We can go out and celebrate if you want. We need to get us a new car like asap, and I think it's about time we moved out of this roach-infestedass building."

Leaving the bedroom Shaila walked like she had an attitude, like it was Darren's fault she'd gotten her ass whooped by Juice's daughter. Darren watched her until she crossed the hallway and entered the bathroom. Then he picked up the Glock that she had just left on the bed.

"No homo," Shaila shouted from the bathroom as she cut on the shower water, "but you should've seen that boy's dick. I thought he had lost half of it or somethin'. He swore up anddown I was deepthroating that tiny lil thing. Oh, my God, it was sooooo funny."

"Yeah?" Darren took the scale and the bag of weed off the dresser and dropped them in the trash bag, along with the cash and the rest of the bud that Shaila had scattered across the bed. The last thing he put in the bag was the Glock. He grabbed his assault rifle and the trash bag and pulled the ski mask down over his face as he walked out into the hallway.

Shaila had the bathroom door shut. It wasn't all the way closed; the door was slightly ajar, leaving a crack that Darren could see through.

"Oh," Shaila said, "just to let you know, I'm not gonna tell anybody about what we did. I know how it goes. My lips are sealed. I'm really ready to do the shit again, to be honest with you. I should've been settin' niggas up. Never thought I'd come up like we just did."

"You didn't come up." Darren nudged the door open with the AK-47's sixteen-inch barrel. The rusty door hinges creaked loudly.

Snatching open the shower curtain, Shaila said, "The fuck you mean I didn't come—"

She froze when she saw Darren standing there with his mask on and his assault rifle aimedat her chest.

He pulled the trigger before she had the time to utter another word.

Chapter 19

'...I strapped the dope to your spouse The first time I gave her an ounce

I put some free bands in her account

Told her, "Bitch, can't be running your mouthBetter watch what you say to these niggas Cause you already know what they 'bout"

Put the game in a choke in a knot

Hit that bitch while I'm choking her out

Put that hook on her, now she got love in the southI got some purp on me now

Stacking the styrofoams up by the door

They done let me back in, now they know they in troubleValet the whip by the front door

On a percocet now and I need me some moreTell me them lies that you want me to hear

I try to forget, but it's hard to forgive Take me some codeine and pop me a pill

I pull on a blunt and blow smoke out my earsI smoke on this blunt, I get high as I can

I float off the Earth in designer

I'm working on having some mannersI'm thinking about it right now

I'm holding the cash while I pour up the leanThen I put one in the air...'

Reese bounced to the beat of Future's "Thought It Was A Drought" while sipping iced Actavis and Sprite out of a double-stacked Styrofoam cup and smoking a 14-gram blunt ofPurple Kush.

The twins were in front of him, shaking their asses in the titillating white one-piece Gucci swimsuits he'd bought for them during last week's New York City trip.

Bankroll Reese had a weakness: a big-bootied, pretty-faced redbone with her hair and nails done never failed to turn him on full beast mode.

Right now he had two of them dancing around in front of him, two beautiful twin sisterswho in his opinion were as thick as Deelishis and as bad as Beyoncé. Their friends — Myesha, Chandra, Tamera and Tirzah — were mere feet away, twerking and bouncing and rocking to the trap music, but the girls Reese liked the most were Dawn and Shawnna.

There were two dozen more bad women at the pool party, but neither of them had anything on the Wilkins sisters. Not to Reese, at least. Though he only wanted Shawnna, he couldn't help but envision Dawn joining in. It was a fantasy of his to fuck a bad set of twins. He'd done it with a Asian twins once, during a recent trip to Houston, but they weren't as thick and flawless as the Wilkins twins. In Reese's eyes — and the eyes of one million new Snapchat and Instagram followers — the Wilkins twins were as stunningly beautiful as Kobe Bryant's wife.

Plus, they were eighteen years old, same age as Reese. For the last two years he'd sat and listened to dozens of men describe how badly they wanted the Wilkins twins, how they couldn't wait for the girls to turn eighteen. Reese felt like he'd struck gold. It was almost too good to be true.

"Y'all sure Juice ain't gon' start trippin' about seeing y'all turnt up like this?" Reese asked thetwins.

"We're grown women, Reese," Shawnna answered. "I make my own decisions. So does Dawn. We're good. When my daddy gets here he ain't gon' do nothing but hug us, talk to you, and leave. Might stay a while for the food and liquor, but that's about it."

"I hope so. Ain't trying to be gettin' into it with the big homie. He used to be my daddy's right-hand man. Gotta respect that bond forever."

Reese took another sip of Lean. He had just hung up from talking with Juice, who would be arriving here at the Villa Taj any minute now. All Juice had told him was that they needed to have an important talk. Reese hoped it was about some dope. Uncle Kevin was apparently in direneed of more cocaine to make money in North Lawndale. Reese was making sure Kev was eating, but Kev wanted to start getting big money, not just the $10,000-$20,000 he made overseeing Juice's packages. The occasional $10,000 Reese usually gave Kev every month or so apparently wasn't enough. He wanted more, and Reese didn't blame him for the ambition.

There was a chaise lounge directly behind Reese. He sat down on the foot of it and passed his blunt to Chubb before scooting all the way back. His eyes became stuck on Shawnna and Dawn's wobbling derrieres. The Future song was soon replaced by Gucci Mane's latest club banger "Gucci Please". When Gucci said, 'It's a cold blooded motherfuckin' Rollie on my sleeve',Reese held up his left arm to show off the icy watch on his wrist. Reese's watch wasn't a Rollie;it was an Audemars Piguet, fully loaded with VVS grade white diamonds. He had taken off the Versace robe and his black Christian Louboutin sneakers. His black jeans and T-shirt were True Religion. His belt, shades, and the bandana tied around his head were all Louis Vuitton. He had custom Louis Vuitton cases on his two iPhones, which were lying atop his Louis Vuitton duffle bag next to his chaise lounge.

The one thing weighing heaviest on Reese's mind was how badly he wanted to fuck Shawnna Wilkins. He couldn't stop staring at her. She was a tad bit thicker than Dawn and a whole lot more gangster. Reese loved the way she carried herself. She exuded more confidence than a lot of celebrities Reese was acquainted with, and she walked like she was the baddest bitch on planet Earth. She had a Styrofoam cup full of Patrón, just like her sister, and Reese could tell that she was feeling the liquor by the way she was swaying her hips and licking her lips.

"You like that nigga Gucci, huh?" Reese asked Shawnna.

She turned to face him. One second later Dawn made the same turn. They both smiled at the same time, identical smiles from identical twins.

"Mm hmm. I fuck with Wop the long way," Shawnna said, biting the tip of her straw.

"You know his net worth?" Reese grabbed the blunt back from Chubb, who was seated inthe chaise lounge to his right; Suwu, seated to Reese's left, was busy eating from a plate ofshrimp and lobster. "I'm talking about this year, twenty-sixteen."

Shawnna shook her head no.

"It's $5 million. Mine is $50 million. If you like him, you should love me." "You got fifty million in the bank?" Dawn asked in a conspiratorial whisper.

"Nah," Reese said, "but I'm close to it. I got thirty-seven in there, that I can touch right now. A lot of my net worth is in mansions, cars, clothes, and jewelry. I don't rent my jewelry. I own everything I got. That Bentley truck, the Rolls-Royces and Lamborghinis in my garage, all this bling I got on. All this shit is mine. The jewelry broski n'em rockin'. I paid for all this shit."

"We know you got long money, nigga," Dawn said with a glowing smirk. "You ain't gotta keep throwing it in our face."

"For real. Baller. What, you want a round of applause for being rich?" Shawnna had to addin her two cents.

"Yeah?" Reese put down his cup and passed the blunt to Lil Luke (a dreadlock-headed 18- year-old he'd gone to high school with). "Y'all got jokes?"

"Don't play with me, Reese," Shawnna said, laughing as she and Dawn backed away from him. "You know we just got our hair done. Ain't nobody got time to be playing no water games. It's twenty-sixteen but this ain't the Olympics. You will get fucked up if you try throwing us—"

Shawnna screamed as Reese lunged forward and wrapped his arms around her waist. Dawn tried to help, but it was to no avail; Reese lifted Shawnna high in the air and tossed her right into the swimming pool. She screamed at the top of her lungs as she soared through the air.

Reese expected the other girls to laugh along with him and the guys. Sadly, he was mistaken. Tara, Myesha, Dawn, Tamera and Tirzah rushed him. Lil Luke and Chubb tried to help him. Chubb reached for Dawn but she dodged him and wrapped herself around Reese's legs. Tamera and Tirzah's arms went around his upper body. Tara shoved him as the other girls held him, and they all soon joined Shawnna in the swimming pool.

The sight of Reese splashing into the pool motivated all the other girls to jump in. He came up out of the water laughing. Suwu was doubled over in laughter beside the pool. Chubb popped up in front of Reese. Shawnna, Dawn, Tara, Tamera, and Tirzah all gave each other high-fives and laughed heartily.

"Got his ass," Shawnna said cheerfully.

"I'm fuckin' y'all up. On my daddy," Reese threatened jokingly.

He got out of the swimming pool and went to the water slide, which started a long line of women who wanted to slide down behind him.

This was the kind of fun Reese liked having. He lived for moments like this. His idea of fun was a bunch of happy girls partying with him and his crew. All the gunplay that seemed to defineblack male Chicagoans nowadays wasn't in him. He was young, handsome, and wealthy. All he wanted to do was celebrate life with African American queens like Shawnna and Dawn while making even more money.

He was just about to climb the ladder for another trip down the water slide when he saw Juice come walking around the side of the mansion.

Juice's face lit up when he realized how populated the party was. He looked around until he locked eyes with Reese. By then Reese was walking toward him, drying off with a large towel. "What's up, big homie," Reese said, reaching out to Juice for a handshake.

They did the Traveler Vice Lord handshake.

"We gotta make this quick," Juice said, eyeing all the beautiful women in and around the pool. "I need you. You told me you'd invest when I talked to my connect. Well, he just got at me.He got twenty bricks for me right now. $38,000 apiece."

"What?! Man, he better come better than that. That's too much for a brick. I know a nigga in LA who can get em for twenty-nine."

"Can he get twenty of em here to the city? Because if he can I say we start fuckin' with him.

If not, then we need to fuck with my guy. He got the best white in the city."

Reese shook his head and turned to stare at the girls while he thought over the potential drugdeal. The only reason he was going to buy some kilos was to help boost the strength of his neighborhood. He hated hearing that his old friends were being murdered left and right in the streets, and he was pretty sure that the body count on his side would drop if the guys in his neighborhood had more money and guns.

More cocaine meant more money and guns.

"So," Reese asked, "how much you think I'll make off ten bricks? If I had my uncle get it all off?"

Juice shrugged his wide shoulders. "Somewhere around $700,000. That's if you cook em up and have the lil homies sell it all. Shouldn't take you no more than a month to get all of it gone, especially if you trap it out of my spots. I'll let you use em. Since it's for the hood."

"I just wanna make my money back and give back to the block at the same time. Make sure the lil bruhs got money to buy guns and shells for them fuck-niggas. It's a war out there. I want us to be ready for it." Reese paused, thinking, thinking. "I can't pay that much per brick, though. Most I'll give up is thirty-four apiece. I really wanna say thirty. When my pops had the streets on lock he was selling bricks for eighteen."

"That was a long time ago, nephew. Ain't nobody selling bricks for the low like that nomore. Not even the cartels. It's too hard to get the shit over here. Most niggas out here paying forty for a shirt. We gotta at least pay thirty-five. I'll try to talk him down to that. I know he gotas many bricks as we need. Think he said he got two hundred and fifty of em. But we gotta pay his prices. That's the only way he'll do business."

"Yeah, I know." Reese sighed. He thought a moment longer, draping the bath towel around the nape of his neck. He eyed the diamond-flooded face of his watch. "A'ight, I'll do it. For Kev. Most I'm willing to give up right now is $350,000. Talk him down to that."

"I'll try. But I need it now. Gotta meet up with him in a few hours. You got it all in cash?""Ain't my name Bankroll Reese?"

Juice chuckled and shook his head. Reese waved for Juice to follow him, and they headed over to Reese's lounge chair.

"I got a question for you," Juice said."Shoot."

"Have you overheard Shawnna or Dawn saying anything about me and Chandra?""Nuh uh. Why you ask that?"

"Just asking."

"Nah, nigga, you asked for a reason. You fucked Chandra, didn't you?"Juice didn't reply.

"You ain't shit, unc." Reese laughed and pointed to a circle of girls in the swimming pool. "Look. She's in the pool. That's her with Tara and Tirzah."

Juice hesitantly glanced over in Chandra's direction. Reese noticed a brief smile on the OG's face. There was something about Chandra that Juice liked. It was made obvious by his shift in mannerisms; he seemed to simultaneously become relaxed and happy at the sight of her.

When Chandra and the twins laid eyes on Juice they immediately climbed out of the pooland ran to him. Reese and Juice were just sitting down when the girls reached them.

"Daddy!" Shawnna and Dawn shouted simultaneously as they hopped on Juice's lap. Juice shoved them away but they kept climbing all over him.

"Come on, now. Y'all getting me all wet and shit. Calm the fuck down. Y'all been drinking?"Shawnna laughed out loud. "Would we do something like that?"

Juice turned and squinted at Reese, who raised his hands and brows."I'm innocent," Reese said. "That's on them."

"Don't make me have to fuck y'all up out here. You know I will," Juice threatened, and he didn't sound like he was joking.

The twins rolled their eyes but they didn't speak again. Reese grabbed his smartphones and his duffle bag. "Come on, Juice. Let's talk in the house, big homies."

Juice trailed Reese into the huge mansion's rear entrance, followed by Chubb and Suwu. Chandra tried to come in with them. Chubb put a hand on her chest and gave her a firm push at the threshold of the back door.

"Nah, let her in, bruh," Reese said.

Juice looked back at Chandra, then continued on behind Reese.

When they got to the front of the mansion Reese stopped in the vast foyer. "Y'all sit here,"he said, pointing to the staircase. "I'll get the bread together and bring it out here to you. Shouldn't take me no more than twenty minutes."

Chapter 20

Chandra crossed her arms over her chest and glowered at Juice as he sat on the third step andreturned her stare.

"You're an asshole, Juice. You're full of shit and you know it. Where the fuck have you been?"

"I'm not even supposed to be fucking with you. You know I'm a married man. My wife just found out about us, too. We gotta put an end to that bullshit. Should've never done it in the first place."

"Are you fucking serious, Juice?!" Chandra put her hands on her hips. "Whatever happened to you leaving her for me? Was that all a bunch of bullshit to get in my panties?"

Juice hated to nod his head yes but he had to. There really wasn't any other choice. He had toget rid of Chandra before things got out of hand. Shakela was far too nosey. She wouldinvestigate Chandra until something came out of the investigation. Juice wasn't trying to wait for that to happen.

He remembered telling Chandra that he was eventually going to leave Shakela to be withher. Chandra was right. It was complete bullshit. There was no way Juice was going to leave his wife. Shakela was the most beautiful, loyal, ride-or-die black woman he'd ever known. He couldn't afford to lose her under any circumstances.

Chandra's eyes filled with tears. She wiped them with the backs of her hands but the tears soon returned.

"I'm sorry, lil mama. Didn't mean to hurt you. It was really just all fun to me."

"You think it's cool to play with a girl's heart like this?" She was full-on sobbing now. It wasdifficult seeing her so distraught. Juice fought the urge to pull her in for a hug.

Instead of reaching out to her he mimicked her pose; he crossed his arms and scratched anelbow. His shirt and pants were wet where the twins had jumped all over him.

"I hate you so much, Juice. I really do. I swear to God I'm not lying. I really, really, reallyhate your guts. You're a lying, no-good piece of shit."

"I'm...I'm sorry, Chandra." It was the only response that came to Juice's mind. "I didn't meanto hurt you or lie to you or none of that. You gotta believe me. I just saw you walking by lookingfine as fuck and I couldn't bite my tongue. That was my fault. I'm apologizing for it. I'm sorry."

Chandra flipped him a middle finger before stomping off in the direction from which they'd come.

Not wanting to leave feeling all torn up inside, Juice went after her. He curled an arm aroundher waist and pulled her back against him. He flicked his eyes in every direction to make sure no one was watching, then turned her around to face him and pressed his lips to hers.

Chandra melted in his arms. She kept sobbing but her lips did not move away from his. He put his hands on her pleasantly plump buttocks and gave it a strong squeeze.

He slipped a hand up her back and around to her face. Her long, center-parted black hair hadblonde purple ends, and it was all wet from the pool. Juice thumbed a couple of dripping strands off to the side of Chandra's pretty face. He pulled back, separating their lips. He kissed her on theforehead.

"You'll be fine. I'm not saying it's over for good." Juice rubbed her back for a few seconds. "Just give me a lil while to calm wifey down. I got something for you later on, too. Something nice."

"All I want is my car out the shop." Chandra was sniffling and wiping away the tears. Her sexy red one-piece swimsuit revealed a lot of skin. Her breasts looked perfect in it. So did her hips and thighs. The small tattoo of a cherry on her left hip looked extra juicy.

"I'll get it out for you. Just calm down, lil mama. There is no reason to be doing all this crying. And we're really wrong for even talking in here. My daughters are here. If they find out about us — especially if Dawn does — they're going to tell my wife. We can't have that."

"No, you can't have that. There's a difference. I really don't care one way or the other. I'mnot the one who's married."

Juice chuckled aloud at that. When Chandra finally got herself together they went back tothe staircase to wait for Reese.

Chandra sat on his lap.

Within a mere two minutes Juice's dick was throbbing hard,

straining against his zipper. The wonderfully soft feel of Chandra's ass on his lap had his dick ready to slide into something.

She felt it. Her somber expression changed into one of sexual hunger. Their lips joined forces again, only this time there was a lot of tongue and lip-sucking.

"Quickie right here on the stairs?" Chandra asked as she fumbled with his belt. "Nah." Juice looked around. "Not right here. Come on. Let's find a room." Juice and Chandra got up and went upstairs in search of a place of privacy.

Chapter 21

"I hope Daddy doesn't embarrass us and make us leave with him for drinking," Dawn muttered.

She and Shawnna — along with Tara and Myesha — were drying off next to the water slide ladder.

"I'll talk him out of it if he does," Myesha said, scrubbing her short red hair dry with a white bath towel. "You know your daddy loves us dancers. He used to come to Redbone's all the time when Cup was alive. My girl Candy gave him more than a few private dances."

"Ugh," Dawn said, and twisted her face in disgust. "Nobody wants to hear that. Candy's a bad bitch and all but I don't wanna hear about my daddy getting danced on, that's just gross."

"While you're bullshitting," Myesha said, "y'all need to be taking dancing lessons like Tara did last summer."

"She is not lying, girl," Tara said. "Ever since I put that pole in our bedroom me and Kev have been going at it nonstop. I learned how to shake each cheek, how to twirl around the pole upside down, how to do the splits and make my lil booty bounce at the same time. That shit sent our sex life through the roof."

"Not trying to hear freaky tales about our cousin, either," Shawnna said sourly.

She noticed that Dawn kept side-eyeing some guy who'd come to the pool party by himself, driving a black Ferrari. He was tall, brown, and handsome — like Reese — only he had dreadlocks and a bunch of tattoos.

"That's one of Reese's boys," Myesha said, following their eyes. "His name's Tweet. People call him Tweet Body. I saw him at the strip club the other night. He's a music producer, works with Sicko Mobb a lot, and that new rap nigga from Indianapolis."

"The one from Indianapolis?" Dawn asked.

"Yeah. D Boy. The rapper who just got signed to Money Bags."

"Oh...I know who he is," Dawn said. It was an exuberant 'oh'. She and Shawnna were head over hills in love with Blake "Bulletface" King, the CEO of Money Bags Management. So far this year

Bulletface and Drake were the only music industry artists this year to have albums go triple platinum. Bulletface's The White Album, a beginning to end drug-fueled narrative of the trap life as seen by a billionaire former drug dealer, had only been out a week when it reached three million units sold. Five of those purchases were from the Wilkins household.

"Bulletface used to come to the club and blow so much money," Myesha went on. "I wishwe had him coming through like he used to. A bitch could get a Benz off all the cash he threw in a night. One time he came with his wife. No lie, they got the strippers rich that night. That's whatmade me start working there the next week."

"What's up with Chandra?" Shawnna asked. "She told me she was thinking about working atRedbone's, to get up the money to get her car out the shop. I think she owes three hundred dollarsto the man. You know she's been fucked up financially ever since she lost her car. I'm thinking about just giving her the money myself."

"I'll put in a half," Dawn offered.

"That's our bitch," Myesha said. "Wish she would've told me. You know I'll look out in a heartbeat. She's one of us now. Been with us, what, ten days now? She's a cool chick."

Shawnna swept her eyes around the pool, studying faces, searching for Chandra.

"Where did she go?" She go in with them?" Dawn asked. She was like a psychic when it came to reading her sister's mind.

"I don't know..." Shawnna caught Tweet's attention and waved for him. "Hey! My twin sisterwants a word with you in private!"

Dawn gasped, and her eyes went wide. She tried to grab ahold of Shawnna's arm, but Shawnna was already skipping merrily away, heading past her purse and snatching it up before prancing off into the mansion.

She shouted that she'd be right back and giggled as she watched Tweet walk over to where Dawn and Myesha were standing.

"Chandra," Shawnna whispered aloud to herself as she walked toward the foyer, "you'd better not be in here creeping with Reese. I'll fuck you up like I did Shaila. Play if you wanna."

The liquor Shawnna had ingested gave her a light, care-free sensation. She just about raninto Reese, Suwu, and Chubb at the large staircase in the foyer. They were looking every which way.

"You see where your pops went?" Reese asked.

"I thought he was with you," Shawnna said, moving toward Reese with a mind full of sexual possibilities. "I'm looking for my friend, Chandra."

Reese shrugged his shoulders. "They must've gotten lost. I mean, this is the Villa Taj. It'll take us all day trying to find them. We can look at the cameras. That's the easiest way to find out where they went."

"I wanna see." Shawnna was happy to do anything with Reese.

She noticed that for some reason his attention kept going from her to the duffle bags Chubb was holding. One was a large Gucci and the other looked like the Louis Vuitton duffle Reese traveled with all the time.

Reese had his usual Styrofoam cup full of Lean on the rocks. He'd changed into a crisp red Givenchy shirt and pants with Louis Vuitton accessories and red spiked Christian Louboutin sneakers. Shawnna didn't know what kind of cologne he was wearing but it certainly smelled good. He had huge gold and diamond rings on his pinkie fingers and several white diamond necklaces with various types of pendants, including two Jesus pieces with brown diamonds in the faces. He'd gotten his hair cut early this morning; his barber had him looking irresistible to Shawnna.

He had the same look in his eyes that Shawnna had in hers. The two of them were hungry for each other.

"Let's go somewhere and talk," Shawnna said to Reese. "Just for a couple of minutes. It's really important."

Reese nodded his head. He told Suwu to check the cameras and locate Juice, then he and Chubb started up the stairs.

Shawnna was steps behind them. "What made you buy this big dumb ass mansion?" she asked as they climbed the stairs. "This place is way too big for me. There's no way I could live here all alone. I'd be scared as shit. Too many damn rooms."

"That's why I need you here with me," Reese said. "You gotta think, with me, you, and the ten kids we're gonna have, this house might eventually seem too small."

Shawnna scoffed at the idea of birthing ten children. "This is not Jon and Kate plus eight.

I'm not popping out that many kids. You must be out of your mind.""How about one kid?"

"I might be able to work with that. One child is fine, or maybe even two, but I'm not about tostretch myself all out having a bunch of babies. Fuck that."

"Can we get started on the first baby now?"

"Don't tempt me right now, Reese. I'm on that Patrón. I'll fuck the life out of you."

"Yeah?" Reese looked at her. He had the kind of grin that was obviously there but barely noticeable. He put his Styrofoam cup to his lips and raised it a little, taking a small drink of the ice-cold Promethazine, Codeine, and Fanta mix.

"Don't look at me that way unless you're ready for what comes next," Shawnna said. "Last time you chickened out and got scared, talking about you was drunk."

"I was. You know I don't fuck with the L like that. Only reason I downed that fifth was to turn up with y'all. If it was up to me I'd drink Lean all day every day. My mama always told me that alcohol was the devil's blood. I try to stay away from that shit."

"Well," Shawnna said as they finally reached the top of the stairs, "my mama told me that liquor brings out a person's true self. It'll make you tell the truth, the whole truth, and nothing butthe truth. Wanna know what truth I have to tell?"

Reese's small grin got a little wider as Shawnna moved close to him. She put her lips to his

ear.

"My truth is, I want you to stop teasing me," Shawnna whispered. "I want you to give me

that dick as soon as fucking possible. Is that too much to ask? Because if it is I think I might needto go somewhere else."

"It's not too much to ask. I'm trying to do the same thing." Reese handed his Styrofoam cupsto Chubb, who had to put down one of the duffle bags to grab it.

What happened next caught Shawnna completely off guard.

Reese took her wrist in his hand and pulled her into a massive bedroom with a fresh white decor and hardwood floors. There was a bed against the left wall and across the room there were two couches, a glass-topped table, and a fireplace. Shawnna liked that there were so many windows, and that there was a door that led out to a balcony. There was also an adjoining bathroom; its door was only slightly ajar, but Shawnna could see part of a bathtub. Reese pushed a button on a television remote that powered on an enormous Smart TV on the wall across from the bed. A Bulletface rap video featuring D Boy came on, and Reese maxed out the volume.

Chubb did not join them in the bedroom. He stood there in the doorway and turned his back to them as Reese practically flung Shawnna onto the bed.

There were very few words exchanged. "You got a condom?" Shawnna asked.

Reese nodded his head and dug in his pocket. He took out a Magnum condom and wasted notime putting it on. Shawnna watched him do it. For some reason she had expected Reese to have a big dick — which he did — but she had not expected it to be so incredibly long and thick. It had to be at least ten inches long, probably more. It curved upward, too. She could only imagine what its curvature would do to her G-spot.

She took off her swimsuit in a hurry. Reese eyed her eagerly, stroking his erection. Whenthe swimsuit hit the floor he was on her, sucking on the nipples of her perky C-cup breasts, rubbing a middle finger on her clitoris. Shawnna let out a tremendous sigh. This was what she'd wanted for a long time. Even before Reese had inherited his father's fortune Shawnna and Dawn had often talked about how good it would feel to fuck a fine-ass nigga like Bankroll Reese. Now that it was happening Shawnna had no words. She just wanted to get to it.

Chubb pulled the bedroom door shut as Reese eased his over-sized dick into Shawnna's tight vaginal tunnel. Her mouth fell open when he thrust his hips forward. She couldn't believe that they were doing this while there was a likely possibility that her dad was still lurking somewherein the mansion.

"We gotta be quiet," Shawnna said in a near whisper, pausing between each word to avoid moaning aloud as he penetrated her.

Reese pulled two packets of hundred-dollar bills out of a pants pocket and shoved itsideways in Shawnna's mouth. The bills looked like they had just come out of a money machine.

"Bite down on that," Reese said, with his barely-there grin.

Shawnna did as he asked. She clenched the hundreds between her teeth and tried to keep quiet.

It was no use.

At times her ecstatic moans were louder than the music.

Chapter 22

Juice's eyes lit up when the music started playing.

He was in the adjoining bathroom with Chandra, who was bent over in front of him with one hand on the wall and the other arm dangling limply at her side while Juice slammed his erection in and out of her juicy nookie. Her expression was one of pure bliss. Juice had his fingers curled tightly around her waist. He saw that she didn't even flinch when the loud music started playing.

He was "fucking the shit out of her", as she usually put it, and she deserved every one of the deep, skewering penetrations; Chandra had sucked his dick so good this time around that he ejaculated prematurely, something he'd never experienced in all of his thirty-four years.

The sound of his skin connecting with hers seemed to fall in sync with the beat Bulletface was rapping over in the bedroom they had walked through to get here to this expensively decorated bathroom. Her creamy juices coated his length like a white paint as he rapidly went in and out of her. She was so tight and warm.

Juice wasn't sure how much longer he could last, but what he did know was that he wasn't going to stop or slow down to prolong the imminent release. He had to hurry. There wassomeone in the bedroom just feet away from Chandra and him. What if it was one of the twins' close friends, Myesha or Tamera or Tirzah?

Even worse, what if it was one the twins? Juice increased the speed of his thrusts.

Bulletface continued to showcase his lyrical genius over a drumming beat in the bedroom.

'...Trap and drill, up strap and killThat's the life that I used to live

Now my son's the future like Future's kidAnd I'm still riding, got Uber deals

And my lady's still supa thick And my kids is still supa rich I'm supa savage like Lil Reese

Got a fifty off in this Uzi clip
She suck me off and I lose her quick
You extra soft 'cause you choose the bitchI got way too much loot for this
Can't get lost in no groupie bitch
Have Alexus trippin', you know she so crazy
We can never let the feds know what we know, babyI came in the rap game like D Bo, baby
Dope game, cocaine, I'm talking kilos, baby Plug hit me with a thousand fuckin' kilos, crazyFlipped it now I'm like H to the Izzo, baby
V to the Izzay, Blake whips yizzay
Bands in a sizzafe, a hundred in the Kizzay
Two middle fingas up hollin' fuck whatcha sizzayDiss me? Wanna play? Put ya brains on dis-playGet on some Bull for the day, I got some sick J's Just picked my tool for the day, and it's a big K
Still trappin' twenty-four, ain't never took a sick dayYa guy want gunplay? I'll give it to him this day...'

The music was blaring. The gangsterish drill-type beat of the song set the scene for the serious drilling Juice was giving Chandra. She was practically touching her toes now. Her head was upside down, and she was watching him fuck her with the sexiest look on her face.

Juice kept thinking about what he would do if someone suddenly walked in on him. There really wasn't much he could do aside from picking up his pants and boxers, and grab his gun off the sink, and hope that whoever the unexpected intruder was didn't know his wife.

He made up his mind to never cheat on Shakela again once this sex session with Chandra was over. Sure, he was feeling good now, long-stroking this pretty little woman, but was it worthhis marriage?

Chandra was moaning incessantly, rubbing her titties with the hand that wasn't stuck on the wall.

Juice lost his train of thought for two reasons: one, he was about to nut, and two, there was another, more high-pitched moan than Chandra's coming from the bedroom.

He frowned thoughtfully. Was Reese in the bedroom fucking some girl? If he was, it hadbetter not be one of the twins.

Juice took a step back and unloaded his cum on Chandra's ass. She made the cheeks jiggle and bounce as they became striped in semen.

Then there came a short, loud scream that Juice immediately recognized was Shawnna's. Two seconds later the bathroom door swung open.

Chapter 23

It all happened so fast.

Reese had been on top of her, kissing her neck, her mouth, her chin, while sliding his banana-shaped erection in and out of her.

Then something terrible occurred.

His dick slipped out of her, and when he tried reentering he accidentally shoved it into her asshole.

Shawnna screamed as she jumped up and out of the bed. Holding her aching bottom with both hands, she ran to the bathroom door and shouldered it open.

And to her horror, she found her father with his pants down around his ankles and his penis in his hand. The sight of his semen on the girl in front of him was disgusting.

Her hands swung from her buttocks to her front to cover her exposed privates as she walked backwards, in a haste to end this horrific nightmare.

She made it out of the doorway and slammed the door shut, but not before she saw that the girl whose ass her dad had just skeeted on was Chandra.

All of a sudden Shawnna's throbbing sphincter was not important; she snatched up her purseand swimsuit from beside the bed and ran out of the bedroom stark naked.

Chubb and Suwu stepped aside and watched her run across the hall to another bedroom. She shut and locked the door as soon as she got in the room.

"Shit. Fuck." Shawnna hurriedly put on the swimsuit. "Was that Daddy and Chandra? That bitch is fucking my daddy?!" She was whispering to herself again, though this time the whisper was out of embarrassment.

This incident was officially the most embarrassing moment of her life.

Shawnna heard some commotion in the hallway, and for a few seconds she feared that Daddy and Reese were getting ready to brawl. She heard Chubb say, "She went in there."

The next thing she knew someone was banging on the bedroom

door.

"Shawnna!" It was Daddy. He didn't sound upset, just urgent. "Shawnna, open up this door.

You dressed? Get some clothes on and open this door so we can talk.""Let me talk to her," Chandra said.

Shawnna ignored both Juice and Chandra. She went in her purse, got her phone, and called Dawn.

Dawn didn't pick up. It was then that Shawnna remembered Luke. Dawn and Luke were probably still talking.

Out in the hallway, Chandra was doing her best to coax Shawnna into opening the door: "Shawnna, talk to me, girl. Please don't let this get in the way of our friendship. Me and Juice started fucking around a lil while back and...I don't know. It's wrong, I know. I'm sorry, Shawnna. I'm sorry you had to see that."

A couple of seconds passed. Shawnna paced back and forth at the foot of the bed, wonderinghow in the world she could have been so stupid. She'd seen the bathroom door — slightly open with the light on — as soon as she'd walked into the bedroom. Why hadn't she checked to make sure no one was in there?

Finally, Shawnna managed to conjure up a few words. "Where is my daddy?"

"He's standing here talking to Reese...oh, never mind, he's leaving. He's leaving now. Chubb just gave him a duffle bag. He's heading down the stairs with it. Oh, my God, Shawnna. I'm so embarrassed. I wish you hadn't seen that. Please don't let your mom find out about this. You know how close my mom is with her."

Then Reese was at the door.

"Shawnna...Shawnna," he said, knocking on the door.

"And here you come with your none-aiming ass!" Shawnna snapped.

Reese got a good laugh out of that. "Baby girl, just open the door so we can talk. Your pops just left. He's just as embarrassed by this shit as you are."

Gritting her teeth, Shawnna unlocked and opened the door.

Chandra was standing across the hallway with her arms crossed and her back against the wall. Reese's Styrofoam cup had already made its return to his left hand. He grinned that tiny little grin of his and shook his head.

"We're all grown as fuck," he said. "We ain't got shit to be ashamed of. I mean, it might not

sit well with Juice that his daughter is having sex, but you're eighteen fucking years old. He gottadeal with that shit just like every other grown-ass man with a grown-ass daughter."

Shawnna briefly hung her head in shame. Then her subconscious mind compelled her to raise her head higher than it was before, as a show of strength against the embarrassment. She knew that Reese was right in every way, but none of it took away from the harsh reality of what had just taken place. It was almost too cliche that in one embarrassing moment she'd seen her dad fucking her mom's best friend's daughter, who also happened to be the newest addition to the clique of women she called her best friends.

It was like a Jerry Springer episode.

Shawnna now understood what Chandra meant when, right before the fourth of July fight with Shaila, she'd said, "Oh, I'm more family than y'all know." It hadn't registered then but now itdid.

For Christ's sake, how long had Chandra and Juice been fucking around?

"I should really fuck you up, Chandra," Shawnna hissed, turning her embarrassment into anger. "You fucked my daddy! Bitch!"

Reese grabbed her shoulders, correctly sensing that Shawnna was getting ready to attack Chandra.

Chandra sucked her teeth, rolled her eyes, and walked off. Shawnna's fierce mug never faltered as she watched her father's mistress start off down the stairs with cum dripping off her jiggling butt cheeks.

"She's a trifling bitch," Shawnna muttered. "What kind of thot-ass girl fucks her friend's daddy? Knowing that her mom and mom are like this." She twisted a middle finger over an indexfinger with the hand that held her smartphone. "Wait until Mama finds out about this. I'ma pop some popcorn and watch Mama stomp that hoe to death."

Reese chuckled and put his hands on Shawnna's hips. He moved forward slowly, poking his lips out for a kiss. She turned her head and he ended up kissing an earlobe.

"You just make sure you ain't out here fuckin' wit' none of them broke boys," he said in his most stern tone of voice. "You're mine now. I'm yours."

"Yeah, whatever. You're a thot just like that hoe. You fucked those strippers in New York, you fucked that—"

"Wait a minute," Reese said, cutting her off mid-sentence. "Were we together then? Were we a couple? Because I could've sworn I was single until now." "Now, huh? What's changed in the past twenty-four hours?"

"You gave me that good stuff." He dipped forward for a second kiss. This time he succeeded. His hands roamed over her buttocks before giving it an unyielding squeeze as he landed a third kiss on her succulent lips. "As long as you're faithful I'll be faithful. I give you my word."

Shawnna showed him an affectionate smile. He'd just warmed her heart with his words. She wasn't the most romantically inclined girl in the world but there was something about Reese's words that rang true. She could tell from the way he treated her that he wanted her all to himself. In fact, he'd been treating her that way for as far back as she could remember. When she first methim four or five years ago at the park on 15th and Trumbull he'd hugged her and kissed her onthe cheek. Ever since then he'd been the epitome of a gentleman whenever he graced her presence.

She moved forward into his arms and kissed him deeply. Reese lifted and spread apart her butt cheeks with his strong brown hands. Shawnna had learned during the flight to New Yorkthat Reese used the same kind of Cool Water cologne his father used to wear. The scent of it filled Shawnna's nose and brought an intense tingling sensation to her loins.

She pulled Reese into the guest bedroom and kicked the door shut behind him.

This time she checked to make sure there were no special visitors in the adjoining bathroom before she and Reese got in bed to finish what they had started in the room across the hall.

Chapter 24

"Can't believe I just caught that nigga fucking my daughter," Juice said when he parked his red Cadillac at the curb next to his house.

He sat in the driver's seat and smoked a whole cigarette, thinking over what happened at Reese's mansion, thinking over the drug deal with Hector, thinking that maybe he could stop Shawnna from telling Shakela about him him creeping with Chandra.

Twice during the drive home Juice had unzipped the duffle bag and looked in at the cash. It seemed to be all there. He'd only thumbed his way through a couple of the cash bundles, butthere were enough of them there to convince him that the whole $350,000 was in the duffle, just as Reese had promised.

"Should just keep it for myself," Juice muttered. He got out of the car with the duffle bag in hand, mumbling about kicking Reese and Shawnna's asses. He knew he was wrong for thinking this way but he couldn't help it. Shawnna was his wild little baby girl. He still remembered beingat the hospital when she and Dawn were born. He remembered the first teeth they grew and the first teeth they lost. He remembered Dawn's first words and the first time he'd had to swat Shawnna on the butt for eating his cigarettes (an annoyingly constant occurrence that had lasted well into her terrible twos). There were so many innocent moments to reminisce on whenever he thought about his girls.

Today's incident at Reese's ridiculously large mansion had just about ruined the sweet memories Juice had of Shawnna.

His wife's Escalade was parked in front of the house, but she was nowhere to be found whenhe went inside. It was a good thing Shakela kept an extra set of keys to the Escalade in a glass jaron their dresser, or else he might have had to show up at Hector's aunt's restaurant in his car.

He had the AR-15 he'd bought from Kev disassembled and stored in a carrying case in the back of his bedroom closet. It was leaned against the side of his money safe, the exact same kind of safe he had at Chandra's house. The safe in his bedroom closet had $120,000 in it; the one at Chandra's place contained $50,000 of what he referred to as "emergency money", just in case something ever happened to his main safe.

He took sixteen ten-thousand-dollar packets of hundreds — $160,000 — out of Reese's duffle and added it all to the piles of cash in his safe. The rest of the money in the duffle was all he needed to purchase the ten kilos from Hector.

Juice brought the AR-15 carrying case and Reese's duffle containing the remaining $190,000to the kitchen table. He sat down and decided to squander a few minutes on his smartphone until Kev arrived.

Thinking of Hector, he went to the app store to read what Snapchat was all about.

"Hundred million downloads," he said to himself, lighting another cigarette. "Gotta be some kinda good."

He was downloading the app when Kev came walking in the back door two minutes later.

"Man," Kev said, laughing and shaking his head at Juice, "tell me why my nephew justcalled me and told me what y'all was on at the Villa." The laughter continued, and Juice couldn't help but to laugh at himself.

"I plead the fifth," Juice said, flicking ash off his cigarette and shaking his head. "I'm sitting here now trying to figure out how to erase that shit from my memory."

"It's even crazier to me. My nephew on my mama's side of the family fuckin' around withmy cousin on my daddy's side of the family. I know I'm bright yellow like a muhfucka but this shit got a nigga feelin' white."

"Shut the fuck up with that shit, nephew," Juice said, unable to hold back a second bout of laughter.

"And what's up with you and Chandra? You didn't know the twins was there? Y'all couldn't wait till later for that shit? Reese say he left you alone for five minutes. Damn, unc, you couldn't hold off that long?"

"Man, if you would've seen how thick Chandra was looking in that bathing suit you would've wanted to fuck right then and there like I did. I was trying to break it off with her. She'stoo sexy, though. Had to get one last dip in that pussy."

"Was it good, nigga?"

"Bruh. Good ain't the word. She sucked my soul out. And I swear, she probably got some of the best pussy in the city. It felt so good I couldn't stop hittin' it, even when I knew somebodywas in the bedroom not even ten feet away. Didn't know it was Reese and Shawnna, but I knew somebody was out there. I feel so bad about the shit now. My baby girl shouldn't have had to see that."

"Your baby girl is a grown woman now, uncle Juice. She knows everything there is to know about the birds and the bees. You just better hope she don't tell Kela."

"She won't. At least I don't think she will. She's a daddy's girl. I'm always on her side."

Shaking his head, Kev went to the refrigerator and got himself a cold Budweiser. He tossed one to Juice, and they sat down to talk business.

"Reese say he gon' lay ten whole thangs on me tonight if all goes as planned."

"Yeah, I'm about to go and grab the shit. That's why I called and told you to bring a pistol.

The ése said he'd have some extra security with him, so I figured I might need some, too."

"I can call the lil homies off the Ana if you want me to. We can pull down on ése five cars deep if need be."

"Nah," Juice said. "It's bad enough we gotta pick up ten bricks. I don't want too much extra attention. Just you and me, and this big stupid ass AR. We'll have this big bitch loaded and ready when we pull up. Any funny shit you let this pretty muhfucka blow."

"On Neal," Kev agreed. "Man, I'm tryna see the whole seven hundred thousand off those blocks. That way I can give Reese his bread back and pocket the same amount. Of course I'llgive him a lil interest for doing this shit for me but the end result will still be the same. After this lick I might just fall back for a year or two. Shit, with that much gwop I might call it quits for good. Get the fuck out of Chicago before I end up like that nigga we had to fire up in the alley onTrumbull."

"What was his name again?" Juice asked.

Kev shrugged. "B Man, I think. From what I hear he ain't one of the niggas that whacked LilDave and Head. Think he just had access to that same minivan. He was sliding through on some revenge type shit, hit up the first lil nigga he saw on 16th. We gotta watch out for them niggas. Word on the street is they're coming for the heads. That's us. I mean,I know there's a lot of big names in this shit, but we're the big names in Holy City right now. Us and Reese. I don't think they'll fuck with him. He's hardly ever out this way, and niggas ain't going way out to no rich white neighborhood to find him. It's us who they're most likely after. Keep that shit in mind, unc. We need to start limiting our trips, staying in the house more, especially at night. I hate that I even gotta oversee all the dope spots. Might start having somebody else pick up the bread and drop off the dope, just to stay in the clear."

"Fuck that." Juice puffed on his cigarette, leaned back in his chair, and gazed up at the ceiling fan. "Ain't no nigga about to have me scared to come outside. We got straps just like the next man, and the next man can get it just like that nigga B Man got it. Fuck em."

"Fuck em." Kev began drinking his beer and swiping his fingers across his smartphone."You heard about ol' girl Shaila? The chick Shawnna got into it with?"

"Nah, what happened?"

"They say she got whacked while she was taking a shower in her apartment on Sawyer.

Veronica told me about it."

"That's what the fuck she gets for pulling up on my daughter talking all tough. Hoes get shit,too. God don't like ugly."

"And she was definitely the ugliest swamp thing on 13th." Kev cracked up laughing. "Nah, but on some real shit, that's fucked up. You know it's bad when females ain't safe. I'm sick of thisChicago shit. Let God just carry me through this last summer. Let me get those ten bricks sold. That's all I need. I'm disappearing after that. Taking my wife and kids somewhere safe. I'm staying in Illinois but I gotta get the fuck away from the city."

"I'm thinking about falling back, too," Juice said. "I got a decent amount of money saved up now. I need to make up with wifey. I'm pretty sure a nice vacation will do the trick. She's always talking about how she wanna go to Miami to visit the beaches. Might just pack the family up andgo."

Kev nodded. "Me and Tara thinking about going to Hawaii with Rell, Jah, Tamera andTirzah. A couple's getaway. Y'all might as well join the party. It's only like $1,500 per person."

"I might do that." Juice checked the time and then stood up. "Come on. Let's hurry up andtake care of this shit for Reese."

"You don't sound too happy about it," Kev observed.

"If he wasn't Cup's son I would've put hands on that lil nigga," Juice said, and he meant it.

Chapter 25

Someone knocked on the front door.

Darren gasped and picked up the AK-47 he'd gotten from Big Jay. It had been laying on the coffee table, right next to the Glock Shaila had stolen and a pile of cash.

"Who is it?" Darren said.

"Chicago Police Officer Jacob Thurmond. Mind if I have a word with you?"Panic set in immediately.

Darren stood up quickly but after that he had no idea what to do next. He didn't want to openthe door at all. He really didn't even want to respond to the cop. But he had to do something. He couldn't just get quiet now, after he'd just answered the officer.

The AK-47 would have to be hidden first.

He put the assault rifle flat on the floor and slid it under his granddad's musty old sofa. Heput the cash — two folded knots of hundreds — under a sofa pillow with the Glock handgun.

Nervously, he went to the door and unlocked it. He left the chain on the door, so that itwouldn't open all the way.

Jesus Christ, he was scared.

"Yes, officer?" Darren said, taking in the sight of the cocky white male policeman.

There was a second police officer behind Officer Thurmond, and three more policemen werewalking up the stairs to the next floor.

"Did you happen to hear or see anything unusual around here about an hour ago?" Officer Thurmond asked. "A young lady was gunned down in her shower in the apartment right underneath you."

"Ummm...no, officer. I mean, I heard gunshots, but that's normal around here. Some boys just got shot in the alley behind this building a few weeks ago."

"Yeah...I remember that." Thurmond was squinting at Darren.

"I try to stay in the house. Taking care of my granddaddy takes up all of my time.""So, you were here taking care of your grandfather when you heard the shooting?"

Darren nodded his head yes. "Yes, sir. I was sleeping on the couch, actually, but I wokeright up when the shooting started."

Officer Thurmond jotted something down on a pocket-sized notepad before handing a card through the slender opening in the door.

"Give me a call if you hear anything. We're doing our best to get all these shootings solved but we can't do it alone. These guys are out here hunting each other down, and hardly anybody's talking. We need cooperation from the community if you guys want all this senseless killing to stop."

Darren didn't say another word. When the cop finally stopped talking he shut the door and locked it and went back to the sofa, where he sat in complete silence for more than an hour, doing nothing but listening for more police and looking at photos on Instagram.

A lot of the guys Darren followed on Instagram were gang members. They threw up gang signs, dropped gang signs, and showed off their guns and designer clothes.

Darren could not wait to hit up the mall later on today.

He would stock up on Robin and True Religion jeans. He would buy a bunch of designer belts and maybe a nice gold necklace to go with the watch he'd taken off a dead man's wrist. He'dstop by a car lot and drop about $15,000 on a used Jaguar, or a Mercedes Benz. He'd get the girl of his dreams to finally notice him. Life would be grand.

When he was certain the policemen were gone he dialed Kobe's phone number and headed out the door with the Glock in the waistline of his pants and the cash from the robbery piled up inside of a brown paper grocery bag. The cash just about filled the bag, seeing as how the majority of it was in tens, twenties, and fifties. There were also hundreds, fives, and ones. Darrenhad gone through every rubber-banded knot.

"Bruh," he said when Kobe answered the phone, "please tell me you went and bought something to give Shawnna. We gotta get her pops out the way asap before we end up being the next Breeds lying dead in the hood. Please tell me you bought her some roses, some chocolates

— I don't really give a fuck what it is. Just tell me you bought her something."

"Man, fuck that bitch. Let her stay with that nigga she got. I'm cool. I just grabbed this whip.

I'm about to pull up on Brianna's thick ass."

"Stripper Brianna?"

"Yeah, nigga. What other Brianna you know? I gotta have me some of that. I know her ass might not be real but that muhfucka looks grrrrreat!"

"And you sound like a weak ass Tony the Tiger."

Kobe laughed. "Fuck you, G. What's up, though? Want me to come scoop you?""In what?"

"I'm on my way home now. Just bought the Chevy from Zaniyah. It's the white one Zo had before the police killed him, the white one with the matching twenty-eights on it. She wanted eight racks for it but I talked her down to five."

"Where is the car we used for the lick?"

"I gave it to one of the lil homies to drive."

"What?!" Darren became furious. He'd told Kobe to burn the stolen vehicle. This way there would be nothing linking them to the robbery.

An old man who looked to be about Darren's grandfather's age was walking into the apartment building as Darren was leaving it. The old guy jumped when Darren shouted into the phone at Kobe.

"You ain't that fuckin' slow, G. Please tell me you ain't that fuckin' slow," Darren said.

"G, we're good. Don't start trippin'." Kobe laughed again. He had no way of knowing that Darren was now thinking about killing him, as well.

"I'll just meet you there," Darren said, referring to the apartment where Kobe lived with his new girlfriend. The Spaulding and Trambul apartment complex was just one block west to Spaulding Avenue and one block north to Roosevelt Road.

"A'ight, I'll be there in five minutes. I'm in the drive-thru at Popeyes on St. Louis right now.

Want me to bring you some chicken?"

"The fuck kinda question is that?" Darren hung up right then, as if the chicken question had been too much to handle. Of course he wanted some chicken. He always wanted some chicken.

Darren was more than a little nervous to walk the one-block stretch to Kobe's place. With the gang war that was going on between the Breeds and the Travelers, there was no such thing as a safe place to walk. Two cars drove by as he walked from Sawyer to Spaulding, and he almost drew the Glock both times.

There were seven teenage girls and boys mingling on the corner of 13th and Spaulding. Two of the girls waved and shouted hey to Darren as he rounded the corner. One of the boys — the only one sitting on a bike — shouted, "D! Let these niggas know how we comin'! Fuck them niggas on Trumbull, we still blowin' on that Lil Dave pack! I still got Head in my Swisher! On Black Gangsta!"

"Haaaaa!" Darren shouted triumphantly. He threw up his gang sign and watched as all the teenagers did the same thing. "Y'all be safe out here. Keep that pole on you if you got one, and don't hesitate to let that bitch blow."

The kid on the bike lifted his shirt to show off his pistol. Darren gave the boy a nod and kept it moving.

He had crossed two more squares of sidewalk when a small white Dodge sedan turned the corner behind him and stopped. Darren looked back; the boy on the bike had his head lowered, and his lips were moving. He was saying something to the driver. Whatever was being said compelled the others in his group to take a couple of steps back.

"You got us fucked up, nigga. Get the fuck from 'round here. I don't know no nigga named Darren."

Darren's brows rose at the sound of his name. Frowning, he pulled the Glock from his hip and turned around to face the car.

The kid on the bike — Darren now recognized the boy as Roger, the younger brother of a cute fat girl he'd fucked a few days earlier — pulled his gun at the same time.

Darren fired first.

The Dodge sped off, but it had to pass Darren first. Roger and Darren fired relentlessly, filling the little white car with bullet holes. Darren considered running up on the car as it passed him, but then he realized that Roger was firing a bit too recklessly, so instead he took aim at the passenger's window and tried his best to hit the driver in the head.

He knew that the Dodge's driver had to be hit, but the car didn't come to a stop or crash like he'd hoped it would. It raced ahead and made a screeching left turn onto Roosevelt Road.

Darren ran the half block to the apartment building where Kobe lived, holding the brown paper bag full of cash close to his chest, eyes flicking in every direction, heart racing like Dale Earnhardt, Jr at the Indy 500. He didn't notice Roger pedaling up behind him until he was merelyfeet from the as Kobe's building.

"That was Rhino, big G." Roger hit the brakes and brought the bike to a sudden stop, and Darren slowed to a fast-paced jog. Darren didn't know the kid's age, but he guessed it to be around twelve or thirteen. Roger was dark-skinned with shoulder-length dreadlocks that were braided into cornrows. The dark blue Bears shirt he wore had holes in it. He spoke breathlessly. "They got a hit on you or somethin'. He said to tell you they know what happened to Dave, and that you better not let them catch you outside. That's why I told the nigga he had us fucked up."

Kobe pulled up in the white 1980's model Chevy Caprice Classic just as Darren and Roger made it to the apartment's front door.

"Hurry up and come open the door, G!" Darren shouted to Kobe. "I just had to get down on some nigga."

Chapter 26

"Kobe won't stop fucking texting me," Shawnna complained.

Dawn put one hand in the air over her head and shook it from side to side. "Nuh uh. Forget Kobe. We can get to that later. Finish telling me what happened in that bedroom!"

Shawnna rolled her eyes and smiled. Her hair blew wildly in the wind. The two of them were in Reese's orange Lamborghini Aventador convertible. Dawn was behind the wheel, zooming toward a yellow light at the intersection of Roosevelt Road and Kedzie. Shawnna had her feet resting on the dashboard and her smartphone in hand. They were on their way to the mini mall two blocks ahead to buy some bundles of hair from Cosmo Beauty. The swimming pool at Reese's mansion had done a number on their weaves. They would be doing each other's hair later on. Reese had given Shawnna the keys to the Lamborghini to go out and get their hair products.

The mini mall was on Roosevelt and Spaulding, located just across the intersection from the Spaulding and Trambul apartment complex.

Shawnna was opening her mouth to reply to Dawn when they heard a barrage of gunfire.

"What the hell was that?" Dawn murmured softly. She let up on the gas and tapped on the brake.

A blonde-haired black teenage girl in a red shirt who'd been checking out the Lamborghini from the street corner on Kedzie turned her head and looked toward Spaulding just as a white Dodge sedan came veering west onto Roosevelt Road.

Shawnna's eyes shifted from the girl to the Dodge as it fishtailed in the middle of traffic, its rear end slapping paint and debris off the driver's door of a red Monte Carlo. There were black spots all over the white car. It took Shawnna a second to realize that the spots were bullet holes.

Dawn gasped and put a hand over her mouth. The wider her eyes got the more she slowed the Lamborghini. She obviously did not want to complete their journey to the beauty supply store, which was at the Spaulding intersection where the bullet-riddled car had just escaped.

"It's over, It's over," Shawnna said urgently, patting Dawn on the knee. She dropped her feet from the dashboard. "They stopped shooting."

Dawn was hardly going ten miles per hour now. She had the sports car coasting to a stop.

Several other worried drivers were taking similar precautions.

Thinking of their safety, Shawnna dug in her Chanel shoulder bag and wrapped her hand tight around the handle of her chrome-plated Smith & Wesson 9 millimeter pistol.

When Dawn finally made it to the intersection she and Shawnna looked left down Spaulding.

Shawnna could not believe her eyes.

She saw her ex-boyfriend, Kobe, hopping out of a white, old school box Chevy on 28-inch rims in front of the Spaulding and Trambul apartments. He had a set of keys in one hand and a Popeyes Chicken bag in the other. There were two boys — one a young-looking boy and on a bike, the other an adult holding a gun and a brown paper bag — waiting at the door of an apartment that Kobe seemed to be in a hurry to get to.

"That's Kobe!" Shawnna and Dawn said it simultaneously.

Dawn made the right turn into the mini mall's parking lot, while Shawnna twisted her neck like Linda Blair in The Exorcist to keep her eyes on Kobe until he and the other two guys were in the apartment with the door shut.

"I know that other boy," Dawn said. She found a parking spot near the beauty salon's entrance and breathed a sigh of relief once the Lamborghini was parked. "I saw him at Myesha's party a couple of weeks ago. He was in my face, trying to holla at me."

"Where was I? I don't remember seeing that, and I know we were together the whole time."

"You saw him. You might not have seen us talk but you definitely saw him. He was there the whole time. His name's D. I think you and Myesha might've been on the porch talking when I spoke with him by my car."

Shawnna put a thumbnail between her teeth and tried to remember who D was. Nothing came to mind. There had been way too many people at the party. Myesha was Redbone's most popular stripper. Every time she threw a party she brought the city out. Most of the guys wanted to fuck her and most of the girls wanted to be her. The twins were proud to call Myesha theirbest friend.

"I don't remem—" Shawnna started, but she halted her words as her smartphone started ringing.

Kobe was calling her again.

"Answer that shit and find out what just went down," Dawn said. "You ain't gotta make up with the nigga. Just tell him we just rode past and saw him running in an apartment after you heard shots."

Shawnna shook her head no. "He'll want me to come over. He'll want to know where I'm at. I'm not about to put myself through all that just to be nosey. If you wanna know that damn bad you can call him yourself. Let's hurry up and get in this store before it closes."

"Give me your phone," Dawn said as they were getting out of the half-million-dollarLamborghini. "I'll call him."

"You give me yours and I'll give you mine," Shawnna countered.

Shawnna rolled her eyes. They exchanged phones and headed off toward the beauty supply store with matching shoulder bags under their right arms and skin-tight black denim jeans hugging their generous lower halves. Their faces were, as Dawn was fond of saying, "beat for the gods", meaning they had the most expertly applied makeup. There were only a few days in their eighteen years of living when they had not been dressed in identical outfits; today wasn't one of those days, and if left up to them there would never be another one. The peach-colored Sealed Fresh Apparel T-shirts they had on were tiny enough to reveal their tightly defined abdomens. The Michael Kors watches on their right wrists were gold like their hoop earrings. They weretwo of the most beautiful women in the neighborhood, but Shawnna had bigger ambitions. She knew that together her and Dawn could build their own brands and become millionaires just like Reese.

Worrying about what some bum, unfaithful nigga would do nothing to assist them in moving forward. Shawnna already hated the decision she'd made to exchange phones with her sister.

The sound of Kobe's voice made Shawnna's skin crawl. As expected, Dawn had turned on the speakerphone. "Hello?" Kobe said.

"Hey. This is Dawn. You keep blowing up my sister's phone and I have it so what's up?"Dawn was a fast talker when she was up to no good.

Shawnna shook her head and went in search of some payback in Dawn's phone. "Lemme talk to Shawnna. Is she with you?" Kobe asked.

"No, I actually just left her."

"Bullshit. Y'all are always together."

"Well," Dawn said as they entered Cosmo Beauty, "evidently we're not, seeing as how she's not with me at the moment. I did just ride past you, though. What was that shooting about? And isn't that D who went in the door with you?"

"How you know all that?" Kobe grew suspicious. "Y'all stalking me? Tell me how you knowwho I'm in the house with right now."

"Boy, bye. Ain't nobody stalking you. I just happened to be driving past when the shit went down." Dawn smirked as she trailed Shawnna through the store.

Shawnna felt like strangling Dawn. She went to the photo gallery in Dawn's phone, then to the text messages, desperately searching for something she could get on her sister's nerves about.

She found it seconds later. Dawn had a new number saved under her contacts. The name wasLuke, and it had heart emojis beside it.

"Tell your sister to call me and stop playing," Kobe was saying. "And my nigga D wanna know if you remember talking to him at—"

"Myesha's party. Yes, I remember. How could I forget? He wouldn't leave me alone for like ten minutes straight. I think he's the real stalker here."

Shawnna held up Dawn's phone and pointed at Luke's phone number. "Mmm hmm, I seethis shit," she mouthed silently. Dawn waved her off, so she stopped and crossed her arms in the middle of the aisle, blocking Dawn from continuing forward.

"Tell Shawnna I heard about her and that nigga Bankroll Reese. What's up with that shit? I get my dick sucked by a bitch and she can't forgive a nigga? Damn, I admit I fucked up. I apologized for the shit. What more can I say?"

Shawnna couldn't take it any longer. She snatched the phone

from Dawn and snapped.

"Nigga, let me tell you something," she started. "First of mother-fuckin' all, you cheated on me with the most trifling, ugly, scrawny lil thot bitch you could find. I'm a bad bitch. The fuck I need a nigga like you for? You downgraded when you did that stupid shit. You went backwards.I don't want shit else to do with you."

"Baby—"

"No, don't you dare fucking 'baby' me now. I wasn't your baby when you fucked with that dirty hoe Shaila."

"You shouldn't be disrespecting the dead like that."

Shawnna furrowed her brows, and Dawn mimicked the facial expression. The voice she'd just heard wasn't Kobe's.

"That's D," Dawn whispered.

"Shaila's dead?" Shawnna asked in shock.

"Yeah," D said. "She got shot up on her shower. Think they say she witnessed a murder and the nigga who did it didn't trust her to keep her mouth shut. That what I heard. I really don't know myself. What's up with your sister, though? Tell her to pull up on me. Let me get her number."

Shawnna and Dawn stared at each other for a brief, thoughtful moment.

Finally, Dawn said, "Nah, I can't do it. I just got L's number and Shawnna has R's. We'regood."

Kobe was saying "Wait, hold up" when Dawn reached out with the tip of a middle fingerand ended the call.

"You got Luke's number," Shawnna said matter-of-factly.

"And?" Dawn raised her brows. "I told you Cage has been fucking around on me. I mightwanna get some payback."

"Then why didn't you talk to D?"

"Because he's with your ex, who you're clearly not too hap-py with. I can't put you in afucked up situation like that. Maybe next time. Come on, let's get this hair. And tell me again what happened when daddy caught you getting your lil booty hole molested."

Shawnna laughed and rolled her eyes up in their sockets. Kobe called back twice, but she ignored both calls and focused on finding the best Brazilian hair the beauty supply store had in stock. Tonight

Reese was making a special appearance at his strip club on 16th and Trumbull, and he wanted the twins at his side.

Chapter 27

'...All the shit niggas rap about bitch I've never been wit' it

I'll whip one thousand grams of blow, and tell the junkies come get itI'm as rich as can fuckin' be and I'm runnin' my city

Ran out of syrup but I got a Perc I'ma drop one in my RemyNiggas dissed me and sent some threats

I sent some goons wit' some TecsGot all these jewels on my neck Wit' all these tools, you'll get wet

Same as yo bitch in the sheets, I heard you a bitch in the streets I'll murk you and skip to the G, on Fifth Avenue with my Peeps Or I might pull up in Nap, my niggas pull up we strapped

You think you're ballin' like Jordan, I'll shoot that bull off ya hat Ain't worried 'bout nothin' like I'm French

Yo hoe she kissed my dick in French Swear, dog, she sucked on every inchAnd you still cuffin' that bitch

I ain't for nothin', that's it That's all it's ever gonna be

Ain't never gon' let you niggas slideAlways gon' empty out the heat

Got that hot shit for cold niggasAll my lil niggas cold killas

Whether it's summer time or cold wintersBet a M we got them poles wit' us

Leave the club we gotcho hoes wit' usBeen a real nigga, on my soul, nigga

You know how we rock, how we roll, niggaTell them fed boys we can't fold, nigga!...'

"I really don't know why you keep listening to this type of shit," Chubb said as he sat up in the lounge chair next to Reese's and watched their many female pool party guests move aroundin thongs and bikinis, drinking liquor and smoking weed and hookahs. Chubb was strongly opposed to the surge of violence the Lawndale neighborhood had been experiencing lately. "Andy'all wonder why these lil babies keep getting shot every other day..."

Chubb went on and on about how today's rap music was encouraging too much self hatred inthe black community but Reese wasn't trying to hear that shit. Reese's only concern was that if hewasn't careful he might spill some of the pint of purple Actavis he was pouring into his 20-ounce bottle of Sprite.

It was a quarter past three in the afternoon, and the pool party was still in full swing. Two blacked out Chevy Suburbans — filled with Reese's old crew of gang members from off 15th and Trumbull Avenue — had arrived shortly after Juice left with the money for ten kilos of cocaine. There were ten of them, urban-dressed hood niggas with heavy diamond necklaces and watches and even heavier assault rifles. Seven of the guys were Traveler Vice Lords, and the four others were members of the 4 Corner Hustlers. As had been the two organizations' practice for decades, they were obligated to treat each other like brothers. They'd all taken oaths to stand by each other through thick and thin. With them being gang members who grew up with Reese, the young men were fortunate enough to not want for a single thing. Reese showed love to his crew. Bam, big homie from 15th and Christiana, named them "Cup Gang" after witnessing a broad daylight shootout between them and a crew of Gangster Disciples, and the name had stuck. Their name came from Bankroll Reese's deceased father; Bam had been one of Cup's underbosses, and Reese's crew was the only gang Bam knew of that would give Cup's old squada run for its money. The streets respected and feared them. Altogether there were seventy officialmembers of Cup Gang. Though most of them didn't have millions of dollars in cash to blow like Reese, they were all drug dealers with access to tens of thousands of dollars that they routinely use used to purchase large quantities of drugs to distribute, so neither of them were broke. They were simultaneously a millionaire's entourage and a street gang.

Suwu was in the lounge chair on the other side of Reese. Members of Cup Gang were standing around Reese with AK-47s hanging from shoulder-straps on their necks and Styrofoam cups of iced Actavis Prometh with Codeine and Sprite in their hands. Others were interacting with the women in and around the pool. Clouds of Kush smoke were being sucked into lungs all across the massive swimming pool area. The last of the catered soul food Reese had spentseveral thousand dollars on was scattered across two long tables on the patio. Now there was nothing left to do but enjoy the day until tonight's turn up at Redbone's.

Reese adjusted his lounge chair to a forty-five-degree angle so that he could sit up and drink while keeping his eyes on his iPhones and the surrounding area.

"Suwu," he said, "I'm about ready to get fuck shit with Juice. I know this nigga's lying about those coke prices."

"Nah." Suwu shook his head and took a swallow from his Styrofoam cup, which was filled with not Lean but Hennessy on ice. "Juice ain't that kinda nigga. Big homie raised us on Trumbull. You honestly think he'd lie to you about some dope prices? If he can get you tenbricks for thirty-five bands then you're getting them for five bands less than what everybody is paying. You should be happy. Ain't nobody else paying a dollar less than forty for a block."

Reese's expression was indecipherable. He shook up his Sprite bottle and watched the thick Actavis dissolve into the soda and change its color to a translucent purple. Then he poured the intoxicating mixture over the ice in his cup and took a satisfying sip while he tried to figure out whether or not Juice was playing him on the kilo prices.

Suwu was right. $40,000 was the going rate for a kilo of good cocaine. There were no ways around it. The only thing that bothered Reese about paying so much was that he didn't know what Juice was going to make off the deal. He felt like he was being played. Sure, coke prices were forty thousand dollars per kilo, but there was always the possibility that Juice had run into adrug connect with lower prices.

Bankroll Reese went to Snapchat on one of his iPhones and handed the phone to Myesha. "Record some of this next level shit," he said.

She rolled her pretty brown eyes, but did not hesitate to take the smartphone and record a brief video of him flaunting his gleaming diamond jewelry. Reese was tempted to reach out and get a quick feel of her soft-looking thighs; the little butterflies tattooed on her inner thighs made them all the more tempting, and the way her ass shook as she moved to the music made him understand why she was the most popular dancer at his strip club.

He sipped his narcotic beverage and puffed his blunt. When Future's *Fuck up Some Commas*came on, he got up and bounced to the beat. Looking around, he couldn't help but smile. Just a few years earlier, he'd been in and out of juvenile jails, running the streets with a crew of boyshis age who were all gang members. His father had kept him with a big wad of cash in his pocket (hence his nickname), but no matter how much money he had, trouble always seemed to findhim.

It wasn't until about four years earlier that he'd finally calmed down. Seemingly, overnight, his father had gone from being a thousandaire drug-dealer to a millionaire gang leader. Reese went from driving an Altima to whipping a brand new Mercedes. Chubb often told the story of how Cup's rise to riches happened. During a home invasion on a petty weed dealer, Cup had stumbled upon billionaire rapper Bulletface's daughter. He kidnapped the little girl and held her for a hefty ransom, which Bulletface had promptly paid. Reese wasn't sure how much of thestory was true – his father had never told him anything about where all the money came from – and quite frankly, he didn't care to know. He was just glad that the millions had come.

"What's up with you and Shawnna?" Myesha asked. "Are y'all just fuckin' or is itsomething more serious than that? 'Cause it looks like y'all are a couple, like, together-together."

"Together-together?"

"Yeah nigga. You know what the fuck I mean." She laughed and sucked her teeth. "Don't go fuckin' around on my bitch. You break her heart and I'll break every window in that Bentley truck of yours."

"That'll be the biggest mistake of your life."

"Just don't fuck her over, Reese. She's more than just a bad bitch. Shawnna's one of the realest bitches you'll ever meet, and she'll beat up a bitch in a minute. They say she beat the dog shit out of Shaila."

"Dirty Shaila, from off 13th?" Reese had gone to school with her. She had sucked his dick in the girl's bathroom when they were in sixth grade, but her request to be his girlfriend shortly afterward had been met with a stone-faced denial.

Just then, Suwu sat forward and said, "It's crazy y'all brought her up." His eyes were on his smartphone. "They're talking about her on Facebook. Everybody's saying rest in peace. They say she got killed this morning, on 13th. A chick I used to work with said Shaila got whacked in

that building she lived in. She shared a picture from somebody else's page of the body bag being

carried out of the building."

Reese took a look at the photo and a few of the comments on Suwu's phone. He wondered if Shaila's murder had anything to do with the ongoing war between the guys on his block and the guys on hers.

Thinking it over, he walked the short distance to the waterslide ladder. His close friends Luke and Grindo were standing next to it. Grindo, a deep-voiced drill/trap rap artist with red- tipped dreads and a chunky physique, had recently signed a contract with Interscope Records. His smash-hit *Thumb Through It* featuring Herbo and Lil' Durk was currently one of the hottest songs of the summer. For the majority of their high school years Grindo and Reese had been practically joined at the hip. Then, in their senior year, both of them had dropped out and parted ways. Grindo to pursue his music career, and Reese to manage the string of night-clubs he'd inherited from his father. With Luke being a decade older than Grindo and Reese, and from the same neighborhood, he had played a major part in their lives for as far back as either of them could remember.

"Look at the rich kid," Gary "Grindo" Edgars said displaying a beaming smile as he and Reese greeted each other by touching their Styrofoam cups together in a celebratory toast. Luke added his Styrofoam to the toast, and the three of them shared a laugh.

"What is it, fat boy?" Reese asked.

"Not shit, not shit," Grindo said. "Luke just plugged me in with D-Boy and 2 Chainz. Aboutto hit the studio with them tomorrow and see what kinda magic we can make. Might just remix *Thumb Through It*, even though I really want some bigger names for that.

"Bigger names?" Reese knitted his brows and took a thoughtful sip from his cup, moving hiseyes from Grindo to Luke and back to Grindo. "I can't think of many names bigger than those two. D-Boy just went platinum, didn't he? And he got that sexy ass lil' bitch, Deja. 2 Chainz got so many hits. They'll kill that shit."

"Nah, I want my shit to blow. That's my most downloaded song. The video got over twelve million views on YouTube. The only names I want on that remix is Lil' Wayne, Jay Z, Bulletface, Drake and Kanye."

"Well," Reese said, turning to Luke, "ain't that your job, Mr. Manager? Get on top of that."

Luck nodded and said, "I'm on it." He immediately took out his smartphone and made a

call.

As Grindo raised his cup to his mouth for a drink, Reese noticed the fresh ink on his

forearms. They were the same tattoos that Reese, Luke, and many of the other guys there at the Villa Taj had inked into their skin – CUP on one forearm, GANG on the other.

Grindo saw what Reese was looking at. He curled his arm so Reese could get a closer look. "Had this done late last night. I was in the studio with Ceno from Sicko Mobb, and we got to talking about how the 'hood wouldn't be shit without all the work Cup put in. I'm too glad he was able to get rich and leave it all to you. Had to get this tatted on me and since I already had the tattoo artist putting "RIP Lil' Dave" on my shoulder, I said fuck it and paid extra to get the Cup Gang stamp." Lil' Dave was Grindo's cousin.

"That shit with Lil' Dave is what made me start getting my hands dirty," Reese said. "I can't just sit back and let them fuck niggas get down on the gang. I'm about to flood the block with dope and guns. Every nigga in the mob gon' have a strap and every clip gon' hold at least thirty. You know my uncle Kev is the one who got payback for Lil' Dave. He sent the hittas who shot all them breeds in the alley on Sawyer."

Grindo was nodding his head and staring wantonly at Tirzah and Tamera as they sauntered past in their revealing swimsuits.

"I just sent some lil' niggas through there looking for Darren. They say it was him and Big Jay who killed my lil' cousin."

"Same thing I heard," Reese said with a nod.

"The nigga Darren must've been ready for what was coming. I

don't know if it was him or not, but a couple of them niggas over there on Sawyer fired up the car when my lil' niggas pulled up. Everybody in the car got hit. The driver – my ex bitch Sherri's brother John-John got away, but he died from a bullet to the neck. The other two are at the hospital. I just left there before I came here." Grindo's pale gray eyes could not seem to leave the incredible bodies of Tamera andTirzah. "I sped over here as fast as I could when Luke told me Tirz was here. Shit, man. Goddamn. How did she get so fuckin' thick? Remember how obsessed everybody on Trumbull used to be with her?"

"Used to be?" Reese lifted his eyebrows. "Nigga, I still am." He thought back to the prior year, when Tamera and Tirzah had walked into his office at Redbone's. At the time Tirzah was considering a return to the pole; she had danced at Redbone's back when Cup ran the strip club. Reese had tried his best to get in her pants that day, but Tirzah's loyalty to her man, a TVL gang member named Jah, had prevailed. Now she and Jah were married, and her sister Tamera was married to Jah's brother.

"Bruh, you got it made," Grindo said, slapping a large paw onto Reese's shoulder. "You got every nigga in the city jealous right now. You got one of the Wilkins twins. It don't get no better than that."

Reese supposed his good friend Grindo was right. Shawnna Wilkens was, hands down, the most beautiful girl he'd ever been with. She had the most perfect of features: a flawless reddish- brown complexion, the sexist little pie-shaped visage with deep-set dimples, sparkling white teeth, and full, juicy lips that Reese could never stop fantasizing about sucking and kissing on, and the kind of below-the-waist thickness that made people wonder if it was real or the result ofsome masterfully done plastic surgery.

Thinking of Shawnna made Reese want to hear her Charmin soft voice, so he went to hernumber in his "family" phone and gave her a call.

Chapter 28

Juice emerged from the Spanish restaurant's back door carrying the same duffle bag he'd entered the restaurant with ten minutes prior, only now the duffle was crammed full of square shaped blocks of cocaine instead of cash.

He got in the passenger seat of Kev's SUV, threw the duffle onto the second row seat behind him, and lit up a cigarette as Kev drove off.

Conversation was kept to a minimum, for good reason; they were riding dirty with an AR-15 wedged in between them and ten kilograms of coke behind them, and to top it all off, Kev's driver's license was suspended.

Although this predicament was troubling enough to warrant his full attention, Juice's mind kept jumping back to what had happened at Reese's mansion. He wondered if Shawnna had called and told her mother about him and Chandra. God, he hoped not. Just over three hours earlier he'd lied and told his wife that the affair was nothing more than a rumor, that is was absurd to believe that he would cheat on her with her best friend's daughter. Shakela had warned him more than once since they'd jumped the broom that she would divorce him if she ever found out he'd cheated on her. The mere notion of a divorce from his high school sweetheart was so unbearably overwhelming that he lit another cigarette as soon as he put out the first one.

In hopes of getting the situation under control before it could get out of hand, he disconnected his iPhone from Kev's charger and dialed Shawnna's number. When she didn't answer her phone, he called Dawn.

"Oh Daddy," Dawn said as soon as she answered the phone. Her tone of voice said it all.

She knew about him and Chandra. "You know you done messed up, right?" "Where is Shawnna?" Juice asked, resting a hand on the side of his bald head. "Excuse my language, but Mama is going to fuck you up."

"Mama ain't gonna do shit. What she don't know won't hurt her.

Where is your sister?" "She's on the phone with her boo. We're on our way back to the mansion in Burr Ridge." "Tell her I said she needs to keep her mouth shut!"

"It's not her who you need to be worried about. She's always been able to keep a secret. Me,on the other hand…"

"Don't play with me, Dawn. This is not a joking matter." "You think I'm joking?"

Juice's jaw muscles flexed as he gritted his teeth and sucked in a lungful of nicotine.

"Daddy, you know I can't hold water. What kind of daughter would I be to keep something like this from the woman who gave birth to me?"

"The kind that knows how to mind her own business," Juice said through stringentlyclenched teeth. "The kind that knows that unless she keeps her mouth shut, the hair salon she's always dreamt of having is history before its doors have ever opened."

There was a relatively brief pause. Juice puffed on the Newport long enough to leave a two inch cherry on the end of it.

"Blackmailing me isn't the answer," Dawn said finally. "This is about as messy as you couldhave gotten. I'll keep my lips sealed for the time being, but you have to talk to her. You have to. This is more scandalous than anything I've ever heard. Hell, I might have to contact Shonda Rhimes and Lee Daniels. I'm sure one of them would love to incorporate a scandal like this into one of their shows."

And I'd like to incorporate my shoe into one of your holes, Juice thought to himself.

"I'll tell her," he said. "Just…give me some time. I gotta figure out what to say and how tosay it. But I'm done with Chandra, okay? I promise."

"I'm not the one you need to be convincing. Tell all that to the man you see in the mirror."Dawn ended the call abruptly.

As far as Juice could remember, it was the first time she'd ever hung up without saying sheloved him.

Chapter 29

The resounding booms and bangs of yet another shooting drummed in the distance.

Roger lurched forward to the edge of his seat on the sofa. He snatched the nine-millimeter Ruger pistol from under his t-shirt. He looked left to Kobe, wide-eyed, alert. He looked right to Darren, who quickly disarmed him and set the gun on the coffee table in front of them.

"You can calm down with that scary shit, lil' nigga," Darren said. "Act like you ain't never heard a shootout before."

"For real though," Kobe added as he slowly waved the flame from his cigarette lighter from one end of the blunt he'd just rolled to the other, thoroughly drying it.

"I'll never be scared." Roger picked up his gun and put it back on his hip. "Just not trying to get hit up like my friend did last month. He was riding his bike in front of his uncle's house on Christiana. His uncle was on the porch shooting dice with two other niggas, some Four Corner Hustlers. Somebody pulled up and got to blowing. My friend got hit in the head. Him and his uncle died. It messed up my head, too. He was only eleven years old. I tried to give him a gunbut he wouldn't take it."

Darren remembered the shooting Roger was talking about. He remembered it like it had happened yesterday. The kid's uncle had been disrespecting the New Breeds gang on Twitter and Instagram for weeks. When Darren and Big Jay got word of it, they'd rented a car from a dope

fiend and driven over to 26th Street and Christiana Avenue with a Tec-9 and a 12-gaugeMossberg pump action shotgun.

It was Darren and Big Jay who'd murdered the kid and his disrespectful uncle.

"Just stick with me from now on and you'll be good, lil' G. On Boonie," Darren said. He palmed the nape of Roger's neck and gave it a reassuring squeeze. "You did some real nigga shitout there. You could've just stayed out the way. That's what a lot of dudes your age would've done. But you got heart. A nigga gotta have heart in these streets. If you ain't got no heart pretty soon you ain't gonna have no brain…like your lil' guy and his uncle."

Darren chuckled twice, but Roger remained stolid. There was apparently no humor to be found in the death of his friend.

For the next couple of minutes the three of them smoked the blunt and eye-fucked Instagram models on their smartphones. Kobe had stopped by the liquor store and bought two pints of Remy Martin, one for himself and one for Darren and since Roger didn't drink, they took the pints to the head.

"Man," Roger said, coughing on a chest full of Kush smoke. "I don't understand how," he let out another cough, "Kobe let ol' girl get away like that. The twin girl. She's so bad."

"He's retarded," Darren said matter of factly.

"Fuck that slut," Kobe said. "Yeah she might be bad as fuck, but she's a thot just like the rest of these hoes. She'll be right back to calling my phone as soon as Bankroll Reese and his squad finish running through her." He went to the Wilkins twins' Instagram page and scrolled down the photos and videos. Seconds later, Roger and Darren were looking at the same page.

The most recent photos and videos were of Shawnna and Dawn turning up with Bankroll Reese and his guys. Darren studied each photo carefully. He had a gut feeling that the twins' father was involved in the gang war he was stuck in the middle of. He also had a feeling that the cash he'd gotten from robbing the drug dealer in Englewood was chump change compared to what he could get from Juice.

He was just about to discuss with Kobe the idea of robbing Juice's house when he heard keys outside the small apartment's front door. The door opened, and Kobe's girl Tamia strode into her neatly decorated apartment and kicked the door shut behind her. She was a short girl, 4'10", a hundred and thirty pounds of mostly ass and thighs. She had a head full of golden brown cornrows and a very pretty face, and she still had on her Burger King uniform.

Kobe had great taste in women, and with him being a 'pretty boy' and all, he usually got the girls he wanted.

"Y'all hear about what happened to Shaila?" she asked, reaching back to lock the door. The boys all nodded their heads.

"D just told me," Kobe said as he offered Tamia the blunt.

"Cop came knocking on my door about that shit," Darren said trying his best to sound upset about it.

Tamia shook her head in disbelief and hit the weed. Blowing out smoke, she looked Kobe up and down and realized that everything he had on was costly and new. "Nuh un, nigga. What bitch you fucking that got you rocking brand new True Religion and Jordans? Let me know so I can go and find her. I wanna fuck that bitch too." She glanced at Roger. "And who is this lil' boy? Why does he look high? Please tell me y'all ain't in here smoking with this little ass kid."

"Man, Kobe, you better get your girlfriend," Roger said, his adolescent tone betraying his age even more than his size did.

Kobe balled a portion of Tamia's shirt in his fist and yanked her down onto his lap. He took the blunt from her and gave it to Roger, who grinning stupidly, leaned over toward Darren as he hit it to keep her from trying to take it back.

Tamia's attention turned to Kobe. "The clothes, negro. Explain."

"It ain't shit. I came up on a lil' change. You see that box Chevy outside?"

"Yeah, I saw it. It belonged to that boy who got killed by the police last year. Zaniyah's old boyfriend."

"Yeah, well, it's mine now. I just bought it."

Tamia eyed Kobe suspiciously for a moment. Then she gave Darren the same look. "The hell y'all done did?" She didn't allow them time to answer. "You know what? I don't even care. One of y'all let me get forty dollars so I can run down the street and get my nails done for the club tonight."

"What club?" Kobe asked.

"Redbone's," Tamia said excitedly. "Boy, it is going down tonight. I heard about it on the radio on my way to work this morning. Lil' Mobb, Do or Die – basically everybody who's anybody in Chicago, they'll all be performing at the strip club tonight. And you know all the bad bitches gon' be there, especially since it's being hosted by Bankroll Reese himself. I really wanna see my favorite strippers. Oh, and Dreezy. You know how much I love me some Dreezy. He and Durk are my crushes. I like Grindo's fat ass too..."

Kobe turned to Darren with a knowing smile etched across his face, ignoring Tamia's incessant chatter. Darren knew what the look meant; they were both thinking the same thing.

They had just been presented with the perfect opportunity to finally come face to face with the Wilkins twins. If Bankroll Reese was going to be at Redbone's that night, then Dawn and Shawnna would surely be there right beside him.

Chapter 30

There simply was not enough time left in the day for the twins to take turns doing each other's hair before heading out to Redbone's with Reese later that night. They had no choice but to go for the next best thing, which was phoning in a favor from their good friends at Mariah's Salon. With it being the most popular hair salon on Chicago's west side, Shawnna initially doubted that she and Dawn would be able to make appointments. But then she remembered that Mariah, the salon owner, was Reese's cousin on his mother's side of the family. Mentioning his name got Dawn and Shawnna in and out of the salon in less than an hour and a half.

They departed Mariah's Salon sporting matching blonde tipped bobs and satisfied smiles. When they made it to the Burr Ridge mansion thirty minutes later, they were surprised to find the swimming pool out back completely empty of people. There were two groundskeepers cleaning up around the pool, but no one else.

"I know we weren't gone that damn long," Shawnna muttered.

"Seriously," Dawn said.

Shawnna's smartphone chimed and vibrated with a text message alert as she and Dawn strode purposefully into the mansion through the rear patio doors. She read the text and said, "It's Reese. He wants us to meet him in the underground garage"

"To the Batcave!" Dawn shouted laughingly.

"The sad thing is that it really is like something Bruce Wayne would have," Shawnna said. "I wouldn't call it a sad thing. Wish we had a garage full of foreign cars."

"We will one of these days. Mark my words."

They went to the elevator in the foyer, their sequined Louboutin heels click clacking across the spotless marble floor. They'd only been down to the garage once. It looked like the showroom of an exotic car dealership. Shawnna could not imagine herself owning so many luxury vehicles.

On the elevator, she took a deep breath and waited impatiently for the shiny stainless steel door to slide open.

"Oh shit," Dawn said suddenly. She had her purse open, moving her hand around inside it. "We really need to stop getting the same of everything. This is your bag. We must've gottenthem mixed up in the car."

Shawnna saw that her sister was right, and they swapped bags just as they reached the garage.

It was uncomfortably warm in the backseat of the spanking new black-on-black Bentley Mulsanne. Bankroll Reese touched the switch for the rear seat air conditioning, and cold air flooded the rear passenger compartment. He asked Chubb for music to set the mood for Shawnna's arrival, and the sounds of The Weekend's singing materialized around him. Then he settled back into the soft, two-toned leather and tried to compose himself.

He had a throbbing erection, bulging from the left inner thigh of his black Balmain jeans,and thinking about Shawnna was only making it worse.

He'd made everyone but his two bodyguards and Luke leave the mansion, promising to meetback up with them at the strip club in a few hours. Luke was in the backseat of the black-on- black Rolls Royce Phantom that was now idling directly in front of the Mulsanne, and Suwu washis driver. Reese had told Luke to stay there with him after learning that Dawn had given him herphone number. It was perfect. With Luke keeping Dawn company Reese and Shawnna would getto spend some quality time alone together.

Reese looked up to find the twins walking toward the cars in their curve hugging jeans and glittery gold heels. The way they'd gotten their hair done made them look more beautifully angelic than he'd ever seen them. He had a hard time figuring out which one was Shawnna.

Chubb and Suwu stepped out and around the cars to open the rear passenger side doors for the girls. Shawnna got in next to Reese and pecked her lips on his cheek.

"What's with all this?" she asked. "We going somewhere special?"

"Shopping first," Reese said with a nod. "Then to GAM's. Maybe somewhere else after that.

It's still early." He checked the gold Rolex on his wrist for the time: 6:12 pm."What's GAM's? I've never heard that name before."

"Great Aunt Micki's. It's a soul food restaurant on Michigan Avenue. A lot of celebrities eatthere. I went there for lunch a few weeks ago and ran into D. Wade." Reese slipped a handbehind her and rubbed her lower back, biting his lip, and inhaling the arousing scent of her perfume. "You are so fucking gorgeous. It truly amazes me…every time I see you."

"Aww," Shawnna cooed, giving his cheek a second peck. Her eyes went to his short haircut and impeccable line-up, then down to the five white diamond necklaces around his neck and his strategically ripped black Balmain t-shirt. She froze and gasped when she got to the bulge in his jeans. "You're a horny little fucker, aren't you?" She traced the outline of his erection with her index fingernail. "It's so big."

"Not really," Reese said modestly. "Just eight and some change."

"Yeah but it's fat."

He gave a dismissive shrug.

"I want it. Can I get it right now?"

"It's a free world; you can do whatever you wanna do," he said.

Her iPhone rang, and Reese clenched his teeth at the interruption as she answered it onspeakerphone.

"Bitch," Dawn chortled, "if this ain't a freaky ass set up my name ain't Dawn Wilkins. Yousee the drivers ain't even attempted to pull off yet. These niggas had this shit all planned out."

Reese chuckled and shook his head no. Through Shawnna's phone, he heard Luke laugh.

Shawnna laughed too.

"Make that nigga wear a condom, sis. I got some in my bag if you need one."

"I got some," Shawnna said before ending the call. She flicked her eyes around the whitemarble expanse of the garage.

"The hell are you looking for?" Reese asked.

"My daddy," she replied, "and his dirty ass side bitch."

Chapter 31

When Shawnna and Dawn were pulling up to the Burr Ridge estate in the obnoxiously bright-painted Lamborghini, Juice was getting dropped back off at home.

It was six o'clock on the dot when he plopped down in a plastic chair on the back porch and cracked open a tall can of beer he'd grabbed from the store across the street. Kev joined him on the porch and cracked open a beer of his own. They had just stashed the drug-filled duffle bag in the trunk of an old car in Kev's backyard five blocks east.

"You done got yourself in some bullshit, I see," Kev said. "I told you before you ever even started messing with that girl that it was a bad, stupid, retarded-"

"I know."

"-ignorant idea," Kev finished.

"I know. And you couldn't have been more right." Juice cast a glance at his smartphone. "Kela ain't called me all day."

"Think she already knows?"

"Not for sure, but yeah. Somebody on Facebook told her. Of course, I denied it, but she was still pissed off about it. I left out to meet up with the connect before we could finish talking about it. I know she's probably either at my mama's house or out somewhere with Carol."

Kev broke his hat to the left side of his head, side-eyed a white Infiniti sedan that was creeping past on the street next to the house, and took a swallow of beer. "Call her, Unc. That's your wife. I know she's mad and all but trust me, letting her stay that way is the wrong thing to do. She'll get madder and madder by the minute."

Juice did trust Kev, which was why he dialed Shakela's cell phone number at that very moment. He held the phone to his ear and listened as it rang four times, then went to voicemail. Staring at a squirrel at the foot of the stairs, he decided not to hang up like he usually did when confronted by a voicemail. This time he would leave a message.

"Baby, it's me. Give me a call back when you get a chance. Love you." He hung up and sighed. "Why did I get married?"

"Don't stress yourself," Kev said typing something on his iPhone and offering another glance at the street. "I don't see how you can be so stressed out with all the money I donebrought you this month."

"Money ain't shit without a family," Juice replied frankly, though mention of the moneyhe'd pocketed that month did serve to brighten his spirits. The more he thought about the cash, the more he began to relax. "You do have a point though. It ain't like I'd be fucked up financially if she leave me. I can afford to give her the house."

"That girl ain't going nowhere. Not unless she can take half of that money with her. What you need to be doing is figuring out what you're gon' wear to Redbone's tonight. Your girl Bubbles gon' be in the building. You know you wanna see her."

Juice certainly could go for seeing Lakita "Bubbles" Thomas, the most voluptuous stripper Redbone's had to offer. It wasn't often that he ventured out to strip clubs, but when he did, it wasto see Bubbles. She'd been his stripper crush ever since he first saw her in a Lil' Wayne music video about three years earlier.

"What's goin' down at Redbone's?" he asked, interested.

"Reese sent me a text about it," Kev said. "He got a bunch of Chicago artists performing.

Grindo's supposed to be there. You know that's my lil' nigga."

Juice smiled and nodded his head. "I still remember when he was born. Me and his popsused to be real good friends. He's a good lil' dude. I read somewhere – think it might've been onFacebook – that he had just signed a record deal."

"Yeah, he did. He signed with Interscope."

"That's what's up." Juice's smartphone started ringing. The number wasn't saved in his listof contacts, but he knew it by heart. It was Chandra.

He gazed emptily at the number. "Answer your phone, nigga," Kev said.

Shaking his head no, Juice declined the call…just as Brianna's BMW came coasting to astop alongside the house.

Brianna and Candy were up front, and Chandra was in the

backseat. Lowering her window,Chandra shouted “Oh, so you didn’t see me calling?”

Kev laughed.

Juice stood up. “Didn’t I tell you to never come back over here? Don’t start playing these childish games. Get the fuck on somewhere before you make me—”

“Make you what? You ain’t gon’ do shit. And don’t worry; I’m not that kinda bitch. I was just coming to tell you to come and get your shit out of my house. And tell Shawnna to quit making threats on Facebook, ‘cause I’m not Shaila.” She slapped Brianna’s headrest and the car sped off.

Chapter 32

Shawnna's mouth had fallen open when Reese's fat love muscle first slipped into her, and now, a whole twenty-two minutes and two positions later, her mouth still hung open.

There was a tear in the corner of her left eye. The back of her head was on the rear passengerside door, and so were her knees. He was giving meaning to the phrase 'hurt so good', plunging in and making her moan, sliding out and making her gasp. He kept pecking her lips, but she could not seem to get her mouth under control to kiss him back. The Bentley was moving rather smoothly, but she had no idea where they were. Quite frankly, she didn't care. All that mattered was the second orgasm that was quickly approaching. When it happened, she let out a series of high-pitched moans and clawed at his bare back (his shirt and her pants were draped over the passenger seat's headrest). His orgasm came just seconds later; she felt his oversized penis jerking around inside her, and when he went back to his seat, she saw that the tip of the extra- large Magnum condom he wore was heavy with semen.

Once their breathing had stabilized, they dressed, and Reese discarded the condom in an empty Actavis syrup bottle. He looked out his window, then turned back to Shawnna and looked her up and down appraisingly.

"I'm never letting you out of my sight again," he said."Whipped already?"

"I can't even lie." He nodded and leaned toward her for a kiss. This time she was able to participate. "Pussy that good should be illegal."

"I hear it tastes even better than it feels." She smiled.

"I'll give you my opinion on that later. And by the way, there's no need to worry about your pops catching us again. Not within the next few hours, at least. My uncle Kev is over there with him at y'all's house. I was texting him when you and Dawn made it back to my place."

"Are they coming to the club tonight?" Shawnna pulled out her iPhone.

"More than likely. I know my uncle Kev's coming for sure, him and Tara. Not sure about Juice. Your mom's tripping on him over Chandra. Don't ask me how she found out so fast."

"She already knew about it. Somebody on Facebook told her."

"That's exactly why I quit Facebook," Reese said shaking his head. "Bitches gossip too much for me. All I wanna think about is some money; fuck what everybody else is doing."

Shawnna was almost too embarrassed to admit to Reese that while getting her hair done at Mariah's Salon, she had posted an ominous threat on Chandra's Facebook wall. She told him anyway, and he reacted just as she suspected he would.

"Now," he asked, "why would you do some shit like that? What did that girl do to you?"

"It's not about what she did to me; it's about what she did to my mama. She fucked my daddy, knowing damn well that he's married to her mama's best fucking friend, who happens to be my mama. That's about as dirty as a bitch can get."

"That's none of your business."

"It is my business. My parents are my business. My friends are my business, and that thirsty hoe Chandra was supposed to be my friend."

Reese would have kept the argument going if Chubb had not pulled up to the Louis Vuittonstore on Michigan Avenue and put the car in park.

"Can you do me just one favor?" Reese asked.

"I'm listening," Shawnna said, looking at her phone, and then at him.

"Focus all your attention on us. I'm a boss, baby. I'm a CEO, a multimillionaire. Let mehandle all of our problems. All you need to do around me is spend money and look pretty."

"Sounds pretty reasonable," she said with a growing smile.

"Good." Reese pushed open his door. "Now, let's go spend some money."

Chapter 33

Junior sat, all six feet four inches of him, propped up on many pillows in bed, watching Sports Center on the fifty-inch flat-screen television on his bedroom wall. He had an ice pack on his right ankle from an injury he'd sustained during football practice the night before, but it was nothing serious. Derrick Rose's departure from the Chicago Bulls brought him more pain thanthe twisted ankle.

Junior's girlfriend of the last three years, Christina Hansen, came into the bedroom, her hair wet, and her t-shirt and boy shorts damp. She crawled across his body, deliberately grazing his face with her breasts as she went, and snuggled up next to him.

"Keep your titties out my face," Junior said. "They're talking about what Dwayne Wade could do to help bring home another ring by the Bulls."

"Your dad just walked in on me when I was in the shower," Christina said, tickling his lowerbelly.

"You should've locked the door."

"I didn't think anybody else was here. He said him and Kev have been sitting out on the back porch talking. They're getting ready to go to Redbone's tonight."

"Good for them."

Christina groaned and pulled herself upright next to him, plumping her pillows. "It's so unfair that you have to be eighteen to get in that stupid club. I mean, my eighteenth birthday is literally less than two months away. There should be some kind of loophole for things like this."

"I thought you wanted to go and see 'The Legend of Tarzan' tonight?"

"Yeah I do. But that's only because I can't go to the club to see Durk and Dreezy. Do you honestly think I'd rather see a movie than to see them?" Christina crossed her legs, put her elbows on her knees, and rested her chin on her closed fists. She became thoughtful, then, "Maybe we can sneak into –"

"No, we can't," Junior cut in.

"You didn't even let me finish," Christina whined.

"I didn't need to. People go to jail for being underage in clubs. I'm not about to ruin my dreams of playing professional football just because you want to go and see some rapper." He muted the television as a commercial came on and turned to Christina. "You need serious medication. Adderall...something."

"You're gonna need a new girlfriend in a minute."

Junior smiled and administered a soft pinch to one of her nipples. She was a tiny little thing; compared to him, just four feet eleven inches tall, and a smidgeon over a hundred pounds, butshe had the spirit of a giant.

"Don't forget to ask your dad for some money for the movie before he leaves out. All I have is twenty-two dollars and twelve cents in my purse. That's not even enough for me."

He shouted for his father, and half a minute later Juice was in the doorway."Pops, can I get some money to go to the movies and grab a bite to eat?"

Juice nodded. "I had something for you anyway." He dug in his pants pocket and pulled out a rubber-banded knot of cash. "How's that ankle?" he asked, flipping through hundred-dollar bills.

"It's good. Looks worse than it is. I can walk on it. Just trying to bring the swelling down.""Y'all need a ride to the theater?"

"Nah. Dawn left her car keys downstairs on the coffee table. I'll just take that."

Shaking his head no, Juice dug in another pocket and took out the keys to his Cadillac. He handed them to Junior, along with five hundred dollars in crisp new Benjamins. "Don't ask me for another dime this month. The Cadillac is yours to keep. I'll get my stuff out of it in the morning."

Junior could not contain himself; he hopped out of bed on one foot and wrapped his arms around his dad, embracing him in a bear hug. Juice laughed heartily and gave his son's smiling girlfriend a cheerful wink.

"Thank you so much, Pops!" Junior flopped back down on the bed, smiling from ear to ear. "I love you, man. You're the best!"

"Yeah, yeah, yeah," Juice said, turning to leave. "Just make sure you stick to the speed limit and don't let me hear about you riding around too much out here. These young niggas are blasting at any and everybody."

"I'll be careful. You know I don't hang around with that kind of crowd. All my friends are on the football team."

Juice swung the door shut behind him as he left the room. Returning to his comfortable upright position on the bed, Junior counted the bills in his hand, while Christine put the ice pack back on his ankle and then climbed onto his lap.

"Five hundred big ones," he said cheesing, "and a clean-ass Cadillac. I'm in the game, coach."

"I know, right?" Christina was just as excited. "I can't believe he just gave us five hundred dollars and a car!"

"Wait a minute, wait a minute. Us?" He looked up at her. "Wasn't it you who said I needed to find a new girlfriend? Five hundred dollars and a Cadillac on rims – this is my find-a-new-girlfriend starter kit."

"Keep on playing with me," Christina threatened, crossing her arms and squinting, "and you're gonna have all your windows busted and tires flattened before you even get to drive it."

Junior threw his head back and laughed. Then he lifted Christina's t-shirt and suckled her breasts until the crotch of her shorts was damper than it was when she first came in from the shower.

Chapter 34

At sundown Kobe, Darren, and Roger piled into the box Chevy and headed over to 13th and Sawyer. They were there just long enough for Darren to run inside and grab the AK-47 from the living room and the box of 7.62-millimeter shells off his bedroom dresser. After that they were in traffic, traversing the west side streets while smoking blunt after blunt of Kush and keeping their eyes peeled for rival gang members.

They made a stop at Earl's Fashion – a local urban clothing store – just before closing time, and Darren spent nearly two thousand dollars on himself and Roger. The two of them emerged from the store wearing Robin's Jean outfits and fresh white Air Force One sneakers.

Darren gave Roger a hundred dollars to put in his pocket and the nickname Ro-Ro G as theygot back in the car.

"Ro-Ro-G," Roger said thoughtfully. "I like that name."

Kobe produced a box of nine-millimeter shells, and they used it to fill the clips in their handguns. Darren, who sat alone in the backseat with his brown paper bag full of cash by hisside, filled up the AK-47's 50-round banana clip and then lay the assault rifle across his lap. He refocused his attention on the street as Kobe veered around corners, driving like a maniac while a King Louie track bumped from the large speakers in the trunk.

They ended up right back on 13th and Sawyer Avenue, four houses down from where Darrenlived. A dozen of their fellow gang members had gathered there to kick it before the club event at Redbone's. A few girls were also present, one of whom was Tracy, Big Jay's ex-girlfriend. She walked up to Darren's window when she spotted him in the Caprice; he lowered the window, but made no move to get out.

"Just the nigga I was looking for," she said. "I talked to Jay a couple of hours ago. He said toask you to put some money on his books if you can. I'm putting fifty on his books tomorrow."

Darren nodded. "I got him. As a matter of fact, here." He fished a hundred out of his pocket and gave it to her. "Tell bruh to let me know what's up with his case."

"He told me everything. That tweet he made ain't what's got him there; he would've been out if that was all they had."

"So what is it?"

"It's some bitch named Brianna. She went to the police and told them she was there when the shooting happened, that she saw him shoot Head and Lil' Dave. I heard she's a stripper at Redbone's. If I see that bitch in there tonight I'm beating her ass."

"Nah," Darren said, "you stay out of it. Don't even talk about it. Let me tend to it. And tell Jay I got whatever on his lawyer." He leaned forward and tapped Kobe on the shoulder. "Pull off, bruh. We gotta slide through 16th and Drake. Holla at this stripper bitch named Brianna."

"Say no more." Kobe made the tires screech as he zoomed off down the street.

Chapter 35

Michigan Avenue and the streets around it were a treasure trove, waiting to be plundered, and Shawnna Wilkins did not keep the shops waiting. Using Reese's American Express card, shebought two suits and a handbag from Chanel; half a dozen dresses, shoes, a raincoat, and several blouses and pairs of slacks from Louis Vuitton; more shoes from Gucci, Prada, and Jimmy Choo; and lingerie and cosmetics at a department store. She bought two alligator handbags and a shoulder bag from Lana Marx and a sweet little diamond bracelet and a gold Panthere watchfrom Cartier. It was exhilarating. At the beginning of this month, she had been an average hair stylist, living for the most part off her father's dime, and now she felt like the queen of Chicago! She found a luggage shop and purchased a quartet of handmade Italian cases, then completed hershopping spree at Tiffany's, where she chose a diamond necklace to go with her bracelet. Though Dawn only got about a third of what her sister got, they both came away from the shopping experience feeling happy and grateful.

Reese had made reservations at GAM's. When the four of them walked into the upscale soul food restaurant at eight they were promptly ushered to a table in the back and seated. It was the kind of table that had a u-shaped seating arrangement, allowing the twins to be next to each otherand across from their dates. A waitress came, and the twins ordered fried catfish dinners, while Luke and Reese went with sirloin steak dinners.

Shawnna tuned out her sister's date; the only person in the building she wanted to look and listen to was Reese.

He reached across the tables and took her hand in his. "Now I know how Yeezy must've feltwhen he first got Kim," he said.

"You're too kind," Shawnna blushed. "I want you to move in with me." "Move in with you?"

"That's what I said. I wanna wake up next to you every morning. I want you in my armsevery night."

"That's a huge step, Reese. Are you sure, that's what you want? I mean, we hardly even know each other."

"Yeah, but we've been together just about every day since the fourth. I've been looking for arider like you. I know your reputation. I know your family. Hell, my uncle Kev is your cousin, and your pops is the birdman. The real birdman. Mr. 1,008 Grams. He low-key might be richer than I am."

Shawnna scoffed at the ridiculous assumption. "Yeah, okay," she said, her voice overflowing with disbelief. "Believe me when I tell you, he's nowhere near your tax bracket. I wish he was, but he's not. He makes enough to get by, and to get us the things we need, but I don't think he's ever had a kilo. If he had, Dawn and I would have a salon by now."

Conversation ceased as their food arrived. Reese gave off the impression that he still though Juice was, as he'd put it, Mr. 1,008 Grams, but he didn't speak on it again. They finished eating and left GAM's, every one of them practically glued to their smartphones as they got in the cars. Shawnna posted a photo of her catfish dinner to Instagram and Snapchat, and then recorded three short Snapchat videos of Reese. One of him cracking the seal on a fresh container of Actavis syrup and pouring the entire pint into a liter bottle of Sprite; one of her planting a kiss on his cheek as he sipped from his Styrofoam full of dirty Sprite; and one of him lighting an already-rolled blunt of strong-scented marijuana and saying, "This that PR-80. It's the Bugatti of marijuana."

"You are too much," Shawnna said, laughing as she set her phone on the lap of her form- fitting black Louis Vuitton dress. She was having the time of her life with Reese, and she had a distinct feeling the fun had only just begun.

Chapter 36

The collective mood of the strippers in the locker room at Redbone's was significantly brighter than usual, and for good reason. With all the celebrity rap artists scheduled to hit the stage that night, the girls were certain to make a small fortune. There would no doubt be a wide variety of cash-blowing men to seduce. Bubbles could not wait.

"Twenty-five minutes until show time, ladies!" Myesha shouted to the nearly fifty strippers that occupied the locker room with her. She was standing at her locker putting away her purse and other personal belongings. Her buddy – the much more voluptuous Bubbles – was at herside, and Brianna and Candy were at the wall mirror behind her.

"Word is," Bubbles said, "we're gonna have two Bulls players in the building tonight. I hope they come to blow a bag of money. I most definitely need that."

Myesha – stage name Ass 4Dayz – shut her locker door. "I'm not checking for them. A lotof those ball players don't have it like bitches think they do. Their money's always tied up, or controlled by their wives. Don't get me wrong, some of them will come through every now and then and make it thunderstorm, but I'm more focused on the dope boys. Speaking of which, your man is on his way here."

"My man?" Bubbles hadn't had a man in months.

"You know who I'm talking about. The only nigga who won't get a lap dance unless it's from you."

"Oh," Bubbles smirked. "You mean Juice. I haven't seen him in a while. Wonder what he's been up to."

"Getting money, girl. Big money. People don't really know it because he's so low-key. Theythink that he's a nobody because he's been driving around in that same old Cadillac, but they don't know that most of the dope being sold out here is his. I never talk about it with the twins, but I know for a fact that he's making some serious money."

"And how do you know all this?" Bubbles asked.

"Girl, you know Tara's my bitch. She's married to Juice's nephew Kevin. That's his right hand."

Bubbles only allowed time for the information to finally register in her brain while she and Myesha lathered each other's bodies with a mixture of scented oils and lotion. They wore red fishnet stockings and bras that revealed all their lady parts, and six-inch red bottomed Louboutin heels.

"To be honest," Bubbles said after some thought, "if Juice wasn't married, I would've given him my number when he asked for it the last time he was here. Messing around with Bulletface taught me to never fuck with married men. His crazy-ass wife Alexus had me kidnapped when I lived in New York. I'll never get over that. Next married nigga I give some pussy to will be my husband."

"Girl," Candy said, interrupting their conversation, "me and Chandra just had a threesome with Juice not even two weeks ago. In fact, it was on the same night that Lil' Dave got killed. Don't let the wedding ring fool you. He's a real nigga and all, but his dick gets hard just like the next man's."

Just then, as if on cue, Ciara, one of the newest girls to add her twerking talents to the Redbone's roster, burst into the dressing room and said, "Wait until y'all see the truck that nigga Juice just pulled up in!"

Chapter 37

Done up in Rhodium Silver paint and chrome 28-inch Forgiato wheels, the brand new 2017 Jaguar F-Pace was, according to the luxury car dealer Juice had purchased it from, one of only five in the Chicagoland area. It was Jaguar's very first SUV, and it did not disappoint.

Juice sat in the driver's seat with all the windows down and the panoramic sunroof peeled back, clad in a $435 white t-shirt by the high-end brand Enfants Riches Deprimes (emblazoned with the words HIGH RISK/BALLER WITHOUT a CONSCIENCE), pale Balmain jeans, and spiked white Christian Louboutin sneakers. He was parked curbside in front of Redbone's Gentleman's Club in a spot that was typically reserved for Bankroll Reese's fleet of extravagant rides and the vehicles driven by the strip club's celebrity visitors. The brawny men that made up the club's security team made no attempt to get Juice to move the attention grabbing Jaguar, thanks to a phone call to Reese Kev had made as they were heading there.

"Look at how fucking long that line is," Kev said from the passenger seat. He too was dressed to impress, though his outfit was not nearly as costly as Juice's. The red plastic cup of iced cognac in his hand had been poured from the half-gallon bottle of Hennessey that now stoodin a brown paper bag between his Kevin Durant sneakers.

There were two lines of people leading up to the strip club's opaque glass double doors; the lines stretched way back to Drake Avenue, two blocks away, and there were still more carloads of people arriving by the minute.

"You murdered the game with this Jag truck," Kev said, studying its intricately designed cabin. "How long you been keeping this under your hat?"

Juice shrugged one shoulder. "About a week. I ordered it, told him what kind of rims I wanted on it, put seven racks down, and paid for the rims. Voila."

"Man," Kev shook his head in astonishment. "This gon' be the talk of the summer, watch."

Kev wasn't the only person who thought so highly of the stunning silver SUV. Just about every passing driver on 16th Street slowed to get a closer look at the Jaguar, and many of the smartphone-wielding men and women in line to get in the club were snapping photos of it. A dozen youngsters walked up to Juice's window and shook his hand just to gawk at the F-Pace's rims and interior, and to look at the emblem to see what kind of SUV it was.

To Juice, it felt good to be the man of the hour, but he could not get over the troubling reality of his wife knowing about Chandra. He could think of no other time when Shakela had gone this long without calling or texting him.

"Where the fuck is she at?" he murmured, gazing fixedly at his smartphone and taking a drink from his own plastic cup of cognac.

"You ain't got Carol's number?" Kev asked.

"Nope. And I blocked Chandra's number after we went over and got all my shit." His shit had consisted of five shirts, a hat, and his money safe. "I don't wanna have to pop up at Carol's house."

"That might be the only thing you can do."

"Maybe after the club. I need a lil' bit of Bubbles in my life first. Come on. They're starting to let people in."

Juice downed the rest of his drink, and then stepped out of the SUV with the sour expression of a man who'd just swallowed a double shot of cognac with no chaser. Both he and Kev cut glances at a white box Chevy that had just skated by. They'd seen it three other times since they had arrived.

"Ain't that Zo's old Chevy?" Juice asked.

"Yup. And that's Shawnna's ex-nigga driving it. At least that's who it looked like."

"Yeah, it did look like Kobe. Probably looking for Shawnna," Juice said as he led the way into the club. With him and Kev being already on the VIP list, they didn't have to go through the metal detectors or wait in line with the other club goers. They headed straight upstairs to the VIP balcony, waving hi to a trio of strippers that were just coming out onto the stage.

"Hey Juice! Hey Kev!" one of the strippers shouted.

"Send us a waitress up here!" Kev shouted back as Desiigner's 'Panda' began playing throughout the club.

"And send Bubbles up here!" Juice chimed in.

"Her and Ass 4Dayz are up first on the main stage, but I'll tell her!" the stripper replied.

The club floor seemed to fill rather quickly, and so did the VIP section. Lil Durk and his OTF entourage took a table next to the one Juice had set his cup on. Juice met a couple of them – Wuk and his father Varney, and Lamron Twin – but the others didn't speak; they were too preoccupied with scanning the downstairs crowd for possible signs of trouble. King Louie andhis MUBU gang showed up next, followed by Luke, Reese, Shawnna, Dawn, and several Cup Gang members. Then came Grindo and a lot more of Cup Gang.

After that, Juice lost track of who was coming and going. He occasionally looked over to check on the twins, but once they were joined by their own little gang – Tamera, Tirzah, andTara – he left them alone and glued his eyes to Lakita "Bubbles" Thomas' bouncing buttocks as she danced on the pole while Dreezy hit the stage and performed her classic 'Chiraq' remix.

A long line of bottle girls came marching up the stairs to VIP holding gold bottles of Ace of Spades champagne with sparklers attached to them. The bottles, purchased by the club owner himself, were passed out to the VIP guests. Juice tried to act like it didn't piss him off when, out of the corner of his eye, he saw Shawnna drinking from one of them.

Dreezy's opening performance was followed by Grindo, G Herbo, and Lil Durk's club banger 'Thumb Through It' and the club went nuts. Seemingly, everyone knew the song by heart. Even Juice found himself rapping along to the lyrics while rocking to the thunderous Metro Boomin-produced hit record with his own bottle of Ace in hand.

Bankroll Reese appeared at Juice's side and slipped an arm around his shoulders. "I didn't wanna ask you until me and Shawnna really made it official," he said, kind of shouting it into Juice's ear, "but do I have your blessing?" He sailed on before Juice could answer. "Not to get married or no shit like that. Just to be with her, you feel me? I don't wanna –"

Reese's words were cut short as chaos erupted downstairs, and as the proverbial sayinggoes, bad things always come in threes.

Juice happened to witness the first incident. He'd been eyeing the crowd below when he spotted Brianna giving some guy a lap dance at a table near the stage. Then a girl grabbed Brianna by the hair, punched her in the face several times, and pulled her to the floor. Three other girls joined the assault on Brianna, stomping and kicking her relentlessly until security pushed through the crowd and snatched them all up.

An even bigger problem arose as Cup Gang began to realize that the large group of guys entering through the club's front doors were all members of the Black Gangsters (New Breeds) from off 13th Street and Sawyer Avenue.

The brawl erupted before Cup Gang had even started down the stairs from the VIP section. Reese and Kev went rushing down the stairs with the gang, and Juice would have been right behind them if he didn't have his daughters to watch over.

Leaning over the balcony railing, he peered toward the foot of the staircase, where the majority of the fighting was taking place, and he could not believe his eyes.

Chandra was right in the middle of the brawl, ducking her head low to avoid being struck by fists and the gold bottles that were now being used as weapons. Miraculously, she was somehow able to dive forward and land unharmed on the stairs.

She quickly got up and dusting off the knees of her pants, came running up the stairs. As soon as she saw Juice, she ran into his arms. He embraced her instinctively, then pulled himself back, and held her by the shoulders.

"What the fuck are you doing here, Chandra? I told you we were –"

A gold blur flashed between Juice and Chandra's faces. Something shattered and suddenly Chandra's face was covered in blood. By the time Juice was able to take a step back and realize that Shawnna had just broken an Ace of Spades bottle across Chandra's forehead, Dawn was swinging another bottle.

Juice tried – with very little success – to stop the brutal beat down of his ex-mistress as the five girls who'd once been her friends beat her to a bloody pulp on the VIP floor.

Chapter 38

"G, why Tracy just send me a text saying it's going down right now at Redbone's?" Darrensaid from the backseat.

"Call that bitch," Kobe said as he made a sharp right turn that took them off Homan Avenueand onto 16th Street.

Redbone's Gentleman's Club was just one block ahead.

Kobe pulled over and stopped the car as Darren made the call. "Hello?" Tracy sounded pissed.

"What happened?" Darren asked.

"We caught that bitch Brianna and beat her ass.""Didn't I just tell you not to do that?"

"I couldn't help it. You don't need to be worried about me though. You need to be worried about the Breeds, because they're in there getting their asses handed to them by those Vice Lords."

Nodding his head and gritting his teeth, Darren ended the call and picked up his AK-47... just as Juice's red Cadillac came creeping around the corner behind him.

Christina sealed her lips tight around the head of Junior's dick and winced as it gushed a fountain of disgustingly thick cum into her mouth. She usually never let him finish in her mouth, but she'd promised to let him do it just this once if he would take her to Redbone's so that she could at the very least get a peek at a performance before being turned around and put out.

And so there she was, with her head in her boyfriend's lap and her mouth full of cum. She felt dirty and excited at the same time.

Then she heard gunfire – deafening, fully automatic gunfire – and suddenly she didn't feel anything at all, for she was no longer alive.

Chapter 39

"You like this big black dick, don't you? Don't you like it? Huh? Tell me how much youlike it, Kela."

Shakela definitely liked it. She was enjoying every inch of Carol's foot-long strap-on penis. She had her face on a pillow and her ass in the air in the middle of Carol's bed, and Carol was fucking her roughly from behind. They'd been going at it for most of the day, longer than they'd ever done it since their sexual relationship began more than six months earlier. It had started witha simple kiss over wine one night, and Shakela had never expected it to go that far.

But it had, and she didn't regret it.

Well, at least not until a few minutes later, when Juice burst into the bedroom to tell her that their son had just been killed, only to find his wife in bed with his side chick's mother.

To Be Continued...
The Brick Man 2
Coming Soon

Lock Down Publications and Ca$h Presents assisted publishing packages.

BASIC PACKAGE $499
Editing
Cover Design
Formatting

UPGRADED PACKAGE $800
Typing
Editing
Cover Design
Formatting

ADVANCE PACKAGE $1,200
Typing
Editing
Cover Design
Formatting
Copyright registration
Proofreading
Upload book to Amazon

LDP SUPREME PACKAGE $1,500
Typing
Editing
Cover Design
Formatting
Copyright registration
Proofreading
Set up Amazon account
Upload book to Amazon
Advertise on LDP Amazon and Facebook page

***Other services available upon request. Additional charges may apply

Lock Down Publications
P.O. Box 944
Stockbridge, GA 30281-9998

The Brick Man

Phone # 470 303-9761

Submission Guideline

Submit the first three chapters of your completed manuscript to ldpsubmissions@gmail.com, subject line: Your book's title. The manuscript must be in a .doc file and sent as an attachment. Document should be in Times New Roman, double spaced and in size 12 font. Also, provide your synopsis and full contact information. If sending multiple submissions, they must each be in a separate email.

Have a story but no way to send it electronically? You can still submit to LDP/Ca$h Presents. Send in the first three chapters, written or typed, of your completed manuscript to:

LDP: Submissions Dept
Po Box 944
Stockbridge, Ga 30281

DO NOT send original manuscript. Must be a duplicate.

Provide your synopsis and a cover letter containing your full contact information.

Thanks for considering LDP and Ca$h Presents.

NEW RELEASES

AN UNFORESEEN LOVE 2 by MEESHA
KING OF THE TRENCHES by GHOST & TRANAY ADAMS
A DOPEBOY'S DREAM by ROMELL TUKES
MONEY MAFIA by JIBRIL WILLIAMS
QUEEN OF THE ZOO by BLACK MIGO
MOB TIES 4 by SAYNOMORE
THE BRICK MAN by KING RIO

Coming Soon from Lock Down Publications/Ca$h Presents

BLOOD OF A BOSS **VI**

SHADOWS OF THE GAME II

TRAP BASTARD II

By **Askari**

LOYAL TO THE GAME **IV**

By **T.J. & Jelissa**

IF TRUE SAVAGE **VIII**

MIDNIGHT CARTEL IV

DOPE BOY MAGIC IV

CITY OF KINGZ III

NIGHTMARE ON SILENT AVE II

By **Chris Green**

BLAST FOR ME **III**

A SAVAGE DOPEBOY III

CUTTHROAT MAFIA III

DUFFLE BAG CARTEL VII

HEARTLESS GOON VI

By **Ghost**

A HUSTLER'S DECEIT III

KILL ZONE II

BAE BELONGS TO ME III

By **Aryanna**

COKE KINGS V

KING OF THE TRAP III

By **T.J. Edwards**

GORILLAZ IN THE BAY V

3X KRAZY III

De'Kari

KINGPIN KILLAZ IV

STREET KINGS III

PAID IN BLOOD III

CARTEL KILLAZ IV

DOPE GODS III

Hood Rich

SINS OF A HUSTLA II

ASAD

RICH $AVAGE II

By Troublesome

YAYO V

Bred In The Game 2

S. Allen

CREAM III

By Yolanda Moore

SON OF A DOPE FIEND III

HEAVEN GOT A GHETTO II

By Renta

LOYALTY AIN'T PROMISED III

By Keith Williams

I'M NOTHING WITHOUT HIS LOVE II

SINS OF A THUG II

TO THE THUG I LOVED BEFORE II

By Monet Dragun

QUIET MONEY IV

EXTENDED CLIP III

THUG LIFE IV

By **Trai'Quan**

THE STREETS MADE ME IV

By **Larry D. Wright**

IF YOU CROSS ME ONCE II

By **Anthony Fields**

THE STREETS WILL NEVER CLOSE II

By K'ajji

HARD AND RUTHLESS III

THE BILLIONAIRE BENTLEYS II

Von Diesel

KILLA KOUNTY II

By Khufu

MONEY GAME II

By Smoove Dolla

A GANGSTA'S KARMA II

By FLAME

JACK BOYZ VERSUS DOPE BOYZ

A DOPEBOY'S DREAM III

By Romell Tukes

MURDA WAS THE CASE II

Elijah R. Freeman

THE STREETS NEVER LET GO II

By Robert Baptiste

AN UNFORESEEN LOVE III

By **Meesha**

KING OF THE TRENCHES II
by **GHOST & TRANAY ADAMS**

MONEY MAFIA

By **Jibril Williams**

QUEEN OF THE ZOO II

By **Black Migo**

THE BRICK MAN II

By King Rio

Available Now

RESTRAINING ORDER **I & II**

By **CA$H & Coffee**

LOVE KNOWS NO BOUNDARIES **I II & III**

By **Coffee**

RAISED AS A GOON I, II, III & IV

BRED BY THE SLUMS I, II, III

BLAST FOR ME I & II

ROTTEN TO THE CORE I II III

A BRONX TALE I, II, III

DUFFLE BAG CARTEL I II III IV V VI

HEARTLESS GOON I II III IV V

A SAVAGE DOPEBOY I II

DRUG LORDS I II III

CUTTHROAT MAFIA I II

KING OF THE TRENCHES

By **Ghost**

LAY IT DOWN **I & II**

LAST OF A DYING BREED I II

BLOOD STAINS OF A SHOTTA I & II III

By **Jamaica**

LOYAL TO THE GAME I II III

LIFE OF SIN I, II III

By **TJ & Jelissa**

BLOODY COMMAS I & II

SKI MASK CARTEL I II & III

KING OF NEW YORK I II,III IV V

RISE TO POWER I II III

COKE KINGS I II III IV

BORN HEARTLESS I II III IV

KING OF THE TRAP I II

By **T.J. Edwards**

IF LOVING HIM IS WRONG…I & II

LOVE ME EVEN WHEN IT HURTS I II III

By **Jelissa**

WHEN THE STREETS CLAP BACK I & II III

THE HEART OF A SAVAGE I II III

MONEY MAFIA

By **Jibril Williams**

A DISTINGUISHED THUG STOLE MY HEART I II & III

LOVE SHOULDN'T HURT I II III IV

RENEGADE BOYS I II III IV

PAID IN KARMA I II III

SAVAGE STORMS I II

AN UNFORESEEN LOVE I II

By **Meesha**

A GANGSTER'S CODE I &, II III

A GANGSTER'S SYN I II III

THE SAVAGE LIFE I II III

CHAINED TO THE STREETS I II III

BLOOD ON THE MONEY I II III

By J-Blunt

PUSH IT TO THE LIMIT

By **Bre' Hayes**

BLOOD OF A BOSS **I, II, III, IV, V**

SHADOWS OF THE GAME

TRAP BASTARD

By **Askari**

THE STREETS BLEED MURDER **I, II & III**

THE HEART OF A GANGSTA I II& III

By **Jerry Jackson**

CUM FOR ME I II III IV V VI VII

An **LDP Erotica Collaboration**

BRIDE OF A HUSTLA **I II & II**

THE FETTI GIRLS **I, II& III**

CORRUPTED BY A GANGSTA I, II III, IV

BLINDED BY HIS LOVE

THE PRICE YOU PAY FOR LOVE I, II ,III

DOPE GIRL MAGIC I II III

By **Destiny Skai**

WHEN A GOOD GIRL GOES BAD

By **Adrienne**

THE COST OF LOYALTY I II III

By Kweli

A GANGSTER'S REVENGE **I II III & IV**

THE BOSS MAN'S DAUGHTERS I II III IV V

A SAVAGE LOVE **I & II**

BAE BELONGS TO ME I II

A HUSTLER'S DECEIT I, II, III

WHAT BAD BITCHES DO I, II, III

SOUL OF A MONSTER I II III

KILL ZONE

A DOPE BOY'S QUEEN I II III

By **Aryanna**

A KINGPIN'S AMBITON

A KINGPIN'S AMBITION **II**

I MURDER FOR THE DOUGH

By **Ambitious**

TRUE SAVAGE I II III IV V VI VII

DOPE BOY MAGIC I, II, III

MIDNIGHT CARTEL I II III

CITY OF KINGZ I II

NIGHTMARE ON SILENT AVE

By **Chris Green**

A DOPEBOY'S PRAYER

By **Eddie "Wolf" Lee**

THE KING CARTEL **I, II & III**

By **Frank Gresham**

THESE NIGGAS AIN'T LOYAL **I, II & III**

By **Nikki Tee**

GANGSTA SHYT **I II &III**

By **CATO**

THE ULTIMATE BETRAYAL

By **Phoenix**

BOSS'N UP **I , II & III**

By **Royal Nicole**

I LOVE YOU TO DEATH

By **Destiny J**

I RIDE FOR MY HITTA

I STILL RIDE FOR MY HITTA

By **Misty Holt**

LOVE & CHASIN' PAPER

By **Qay Crockett**

TO DIE IN VAIN

SINS OF A HUSTLA

By **ASAD**

BROOKLYN HUSTLAZ

By **Boogsy Morina**

BROOKLYN ON LOCK I & II

By **Sonovia**

GANGSTA CITY

By **Teddy Duke**

A DRUG KING AND HIS DIAMOND I & II III

A DOPEMAN'S RICHES

HER MAN, MINE'S TOO I, II

CASH MONEY HO'S

THE WIFEY I USED TO BE I II

By Nicole Goosby

TRAPHOUSE KING **I II & III**

KINGPIN KILLAZ I II III

STREET KINGS I II

PAID IN BLOOD **I II**

CARTEL KILLAZ I II III

DOPE GODS I II

By **Hood Rich**

LIPSTICK KILLAH **I, II, III**

CRIME OF PASSION I II & III

FRIEND OR FOE I II III

By **Mimi**

STEADY MOBBN' **I, II, III**

THE STREETS STAINED MY SOUL I II

By **Marcellus Allen**

WHO SHOT YA **I, II, III**

SON OF A DOPE FIEND I II

HEAVEN GOT A GHETTO

Renta

GORILLAZ IN THE BAY **I II III IV**

TEARS OF A GANGSTA I II

3X KRAZY I II

DE'KARI

TRIGGADALE I II III

MURDAROBER WAS THE CASE

Elijah R. Freeman

GOD BLESS THE TRAPPERS I, II, III

THESE SCANDALOUS STREETS I, II, III

FEAR MY GANGSTA I, II, III IV, V

THESE STREETS DON'T LOVE NOBODY I, II

BURY ME A G I, II, III, IV, V

A GANGSTA'S EMPIRE I, II, III, IV

THE DOPEMAN'S BODYGAURD I II

THE REALEST KILLAZ I II III

THE LAST OF THE OGS I II III

Tranay Adams

THE STREETS ARE CALLING

Duquie Wilson

MARRIED TO A BOSS I II III

By Destiny Skai & Chris Green

KINGZ OF THE GAME I II III IV V

Playa Ray

SLAUGHTER GANG I II III

RUTHLESS HEART I II III

By Willie Slaughter

FUK SHYT

By Blakk Diamond

DON'T F#CK WITH MY HEART I II

By Linnea

ADDICTED TO THE DRAMA I II III

IN THE ARM OF HIS BOSS II

By Jamila

YAYO I II III IV

A SHOOTER'S AMBITION I II

BRED IN THE GAME

By S. Allen

TRAP GOD I II III

RICH $AVAGE

By Troublesome

FOREVER GANGSTA

GLOCKS ON SATIN SHEETS I II

By Adrian Dulan

TOE TAGZ I II III

LEVELS TO THIS SHYT I II

By Ah'Million

KINGPIN DREAMS I II III

By Paper Boi Rari

CONFESSIONS OF A GANGSTA I II III IV

By Nicholas Lock

I'M NOTHING WITHOUT HIS LOVE

SINS OF A THUG

TO THE THUG I LOVED BEFORE

By Monet Dragun

CAUGHT UP IN THE LIFE I II III

THE STREETS NEVER LET GO

By Robert Baptiste

NEW TO THE GAME I II III

MONEY, MURDER & MEMORIES I II III

By **Malik D. Rice**

LIFE OF A SAVAGE I II III

A GANGSTA'S QUR'AN I II III

MURDA SEASON I II III

GANGLAND CARTEL I II III

CHI'RAQ GANGSTAS I II III

KILLERS ON ELM STREET I II III

JACK BOYZ N DA BRONX I II III

A DOPEBOY'S DREAM I II

By **Romell Tukes**

LOYALTY AIN'T PROMISED I II

By Keith Williams

QUIET MONEY I II III

THUG LIFE I II III

EXTENDED CLIP I II

By **Trai'Quan**

THE STREETS MADE ME I II III

By **Larry D. Wright**

THE ULTIMATE SACRIFICE I, II, III, IV, V, VI

KHADIFI

IF YOU CROSS ME ONCE

ANGEL I II

IN THE BLINK OF AN EYE

By **Anthony Fields**

THE LIFE OF A HOOD STAR

By Ca$h & Rashia Wilson

THE STREETS WILL NEVER CLOSE

By K'ajji

CREAM I II

By Yolanda Moore

NIGHTMARES OF A HUSTLA I II III